I0737617

CYNTHIA HICKEY

CHOCOLATE-COVERED CRIME

CYNTHIA HICKEY

DEDICATION

To God who gives me the inspiration, to my husband, Tom, for his unfailing support, to my children for believing I can do this, and to the fans who eagerly awaited the third book.

Thank you.

1

If she messes this up, I'll. . ." Aunt Eunice frowned. The lines on each side of her mouth deepened.

"What? Kill her?" April, my best friend and appointed maid of honor, giggled at her response to Aunt Eunice's remark then turned her back to the store's receptionist. "It's been a few weeks since Summer has had a mystery to solve."

Cousin Mae Belle was late. I didn't know her well enough to determine whether tardiness was normal for her or not. I sighed and flipped through another bridal magazine as I half-listened to background music while Aunt Eunice worked herself into a frenzy. She waved her arms in the air and muttered about the responsibility of being on time for appointments. Admitting to a bit of apprehension, I slapped the magazine closed and rose to peer out the window.

"I told you she was too scatterbrained to be in charge of your wedding." Aunt Eunice paced the rose-colored carpet. "Calling herself a wedding planner doesn't make her one. Also, with your luck, I still don't think it's wise to get married on April

1

Fool's Day."

"It'll be fun, and Ethan will never be able to forget the date. It was his idea. Mae Belle's my cousin and deserves my loyalty." I didn't turn to face my aunt. Butterflies the size of horses fluttered in my stomach. "She's giving me a really good deal, and she does own her own business. That makes her successful. Sort of." I waved my hand around the garishly decorated pink and white receiving area of Mae Belle's shop, A Dream Wedding.

A few patrons flipped through magazines or browsed catalog. "See what she's accomplished?"

I shifted my attention as Aunt Eunice waved a fistful of baby blue–colored papers in April's face. "I won't let anyone mess up Summer's special day. Lord knows I thought this day would never come."

"Gee, thanks for the vote of confidence."

At that moment, Mae Belle shoved her way through the glass doors, her face creased with worry. "Sorry. Something came up." With a thump, she plopped a tote bag onto the glass-topped coffee table, then clasped a hand to her barely there bosom and strained to catch her breath. "Summer, can you step into the back with me? There's something I need to. . ." She glanced behind me and froze.

"What?" I turned my head. The sidewalk was vacant.

"Nothing. We'll talk later." She gave a shaky smile and reached into her bag.

"Where have you been, Mae Belle?" Aunt Eunice pronounced her name as one word. She glared, chubby hands planted on plump hips. "How can you expect to run a business if you can't make your appointments on time? Very irresponsible. Why, at Summer Confections, we. . ."

"Aunt Eunice, please." I held up a hand to stop her. "She's only fifteen minutes late. Not a big deal." I dropped to the sofa and struggled to hide my displeasure.

Mae Belle joined me, opening a thick notebook. "Okay. I'm going to ask you some questions. From your answers, I'll be able to plan the wedding of your dreams. Ready?" Mae Belle took a deep breath after her rush of instructions.

Her attention seemed everywhere but on the task at hand. Her gaze flitted behind me.

I glanced over my shoulder. Nothing but an elderly gentleman walking a scruffy little dog. "More than ready."

"Colors? Are you getting married in white?"

"She'd better be," Aunt Eunice answered, searching my face.

Horror. The woman's candor would be my undoing. My cheeks flamed.

"Bridesmaids?"

I waited a second to see whether my aunt would speak for me. For once, she held her tongue. I answered. "Dark purple. Like the Midnight Blue roses I want in my bouquet."

"Great. Any other colors?" Mae Belle's pen scratched like a chicken searching for feed. I leaned over to peer at her writing. The penmanship resembled that particular fowl's scratches. How would she decipher her notes? After I straightened, her attention again moved past me. "A delicate pink as an accent color. I want the bridesmaids' bouquets pink and white. The flower girl. . .”

Mae Belle's eyes glazed over. That did it. She wasn't paying attention. I grabbed her hand and pulled her to her feet. “Come on.”

After dragging her to a small storage room in the back, I spun to face her. “What's up? You definitely aren't concentrating on my wedding. Seriously, Mae Belle. This is a big day for me, and since I'm paying you, I expect your full attention.”

My cousin's brown eyes swam with tears. “I'm sorry. It's just. . . I found out. . .” She covered her face with her hands. The bell in the store jingled, and two giggly twenty-somethings entered. Mae Belle raised her head. “Gotta go. I have to talk to you later. Okay?” She gripped my hands. “It's important. Promise me.”

I gnawed my lower lip, alarmed at her sense of urgency. “I promise. Let's get this initial interview over with, I'll ditch my aunt and April, and we can talk.”

She gave me a shaky smile and trotted back to the front of the store. I followed at a more sedate pace.

Aunt Eunice had taken it upon herself to flip through Mae Belle's notebook. “How can anyone read this?” She turned the book sideways.

Mae Belle snatched the book from her hands. “The only one who needs to read my notes is me!”

“Besides some indecipherable words scribbled in before Summer's questions, it doesn't look as if you have any other clients. You told us you were doing well for yourself.”

“I am! I was. I keep a separate notebook for

each client."

"What about Edna Mobley's wedding? Didn't they cancel because you couldn't get it together fast enough?" Aunt Eunice crossed her arms. "That's why we're starting our planning in September, you know? To give you plenty of time."

"That wasn't my fault. It was the caterer." Mae Belle's sharp cheekbones flushed. "What is wrong with you, Aunt Eunice? Why are you being so mean to me? I'm doing the best I can."

Aunt Eunice shrugged. "I don't know." She glanced at me then lowered her gaze. "I wanted to have a little more input into something this special. It was completely selfish of me. But Summer's the daughter I never had. Now she's getting married, and we're moving out."

I wrapped my arms around the woman who'd raised me. "You are the sweetest gift God has ever given me." I grinned. "Besides Ethan. Believe me, you're going to have plenty to do. To save money, we'll be doing a lot of the work ourselves."

That seemed to make her feel better. My aunt straightened her shoulders and gave me a shaky smile.

I withdrew a folder from the tapestry-print bag I'd brought with me. "Here is a picture of the wedding gown I want, the bridesmaids' dresses, and the cake. I'll let you locate them for me, Mae Belle." The three women oohed and aahed over my choices before Aunt Eunice snatched the photograph of the cake.

"This is a bit different. What's that on top?"

I could tell from my aunt's tone she wasn't

impressed with the design. "The cake is chocolate, covered with white chocolate frosting. The topping is a solid white chocolate molded into the form of a bride and groom embracing. The roses can be dry brushed with my wedding colors. I want them tipped with pink and purple."

"Kind of modern, isn't it?"

I grabbed the paper from Aunt Eunice's hand. "Ethan likes chocolate, and I want something beautiful but different."

"It's gorgeous." April took the paper. "But not as gorgeous as this dress! Who's the designer?"

"Demetrios."

"It won't work." April and I both swiveled to glare at my aunt. "You may be a little thing, Summer, but your bosom will spill out of the top of that. Look how tight the bodice is. You won't be able to breathe."

"I will not spill out." I clutched the photo of my dream dress to my chest and recited the details I'd committed to memory. "A heavily beaded, strapless bodice with a gathered, pull-up skirt and chapel train." April's sigh equaled my own.

"It's perfect. And Ethan will be wearing a tux by Ralph Lauren. I may never let him take it off."

"Yes, you will." April bumped her shoulder against mine, causing a heat wave to rise up my neck. "Is there a picture in there of what I'll be wearing?"

I handed her a picture of a simple, fitted dress in a shade resembling eggplant. A belt, detailed with rhinestones, completed the look. "With silver sandals, you'll be beautiful."

Aunt Eunice grabbed the portrait. "More strapless?" She glanced to where the two other prospective customers eavesdropped on our conversation. They turned away.

"It has spaghetti straps. It's my wedding, Aunt Eunice. And you can trust me not to do anything improper."

Mae Belle fidgeted with the strands of hair hanging loose from a bun at the back of her head. "I'm not sure I can do this if there's going to be constant turmoil. I tend to be delicate, you know." Her gaze returned outside. She gasped and bolted to her feet.

Again, I glanced to see nothing out of the ordinary. If Mae Belle didn't quit turning my attention outside, I'd get whiplash. I glared at her. She wouldn't meet my eyes. I decided to get rid of the audience and find out what was troubling the trembling woman in front of me. Always pale, Mae Belle now looked as if she'd seen a ghost.

Her hands shook as she repacked her things into her oversize bag. Aunt Eunice's harping and unhappiness about being ushered from the store early didn't help. Other than a puzzled glance over being dismissed, April offered no comment, no doubt being used to my rather unorthodox way of doing things.

"I'll call you later," I whispered as she bent to retrieve her purse. My best friend nodded and dragged Aunt Eunice from the store.

Mae Belle jumped when I laid a hand on her shoulder.

"What's going on?" I took her by the arm.

"Let's go in the back."

She shook her head. "I can't talk here." Mae Belle paced the floor and stopped abruptly, her eyes wide and dark. "Meet me at the diner. No, Grandma's Story Corner. Thirty minutes. I've got to get rid of these other customers."

"Okay." I retrieved my tote bag and, with a glance behind me, left the boutique. Grandma's Story Corner sat one block over in a renovated brick storefront. The coffee and pastry bar, as well as rows and rows of books, made it one of my favorite places to hang out.

My mouth watered in anticipation of a vente-sized iced mocha with whipped cream. My happy mood disappeared when I saw the long line.

I forced back a groan and took my place behind a couple of giggling teenagers discussing the latest tabloid article of who dated whom. Several minutes later, my hand wrapped around an icy, cold-flavored coffee.

I found an isolated table and sat down to wait for my cousin who, again, ran late. Really, at thirty-five years old, she should have better manners. If this was normal behavior on her part, I'd need to question the wisdom of hiring her as my wedding planner.

The owner of the store was anything but grandma-like with her dyed, spiked hair and leopard-print leggings. Her stiletto heels clacked on the wooden floor as she strode up to my table. "Looking for another book on crime solving, Summer? How's the book coming?"

"Not good." I winced at her question. I had yet

to start the book I'd said I was writing to cover my reason for buying the crime-solving books awhile back. "I'm waiting for my cousin."

"The handsome sheriff ?"

"No, Mae Belle. She's my wedding planner."

"Oh. Good luck on that. She hasn't left a line of happy customers." The woman waved a hand and continued on her way.

I glanced at my watch. Where could Mae Belle be? Now twenty past the appointed thirty minutes, I admitted to a certain amount of fear. Grabbing my drink and bag, I rose and headed back to A Dream Wedding.

The store still seemed to be full of looky-loos rather than people actually interested in hiring my cousin. The woman behind the register pointed me to Mae Belle's office.

Adopting the same air of annoyance my aunt portrayed earlier, I marched to the office and knocked on the door. Receiving no answer, I turned the knob and stepped inside.

Lying face down, legs straight with a sensible black pump missing from one foot, lay Mae Belle. An ornate-handled letter opener protruded from the center of her back.

2

Every fiber of my being wanted to rush to my cousin's side, help her to her feet, and tell her to lay off the dramatics. We weren't in high school anymore.

I'd seen my fair share of death in the past month or so and messed up enough crime scenes to get myself thrown in jail for a night, so I knew not to touch anything. But I had to check. I knelt beside her and felt for a pulse in her neck.

A moan escaped her. Ripples of warm air brushed against my wrist. I scuttled backward and screamed.

Mae Belle's secretary/receptionist, a big-boned girl by the name of Sherry, waddled into the office and speared me with an emerald green gaze. "What did you do?"

"Instead of accusing me, you need to call the police. And an ambulance." I pulled free a strand of hair stuck to the corner of Mae Belle's mouth. She was pale, and crimson spread beneath her and stained the rose-colored rug. "Mae Belle. Can you hear me?"

She groaned again. Since Sherry still hadn't

moved, I stretched my arm to grab the phone from the desk and dialed 911. The other woman still glared at me. Keeping my gaze focused on her unfriendly one, I reported the scene around me then held the receiver to my shoulder.

"What are you staring at?" I hissed and pressed the phone against me to prevent the operator from hearing. "There's destruction and death everywhere you go. I've read the papers. I know all about you and your attempts at crime solving. Things too slow around here for you? Trying to drum up some excitement?" Sherry spit the words at me.

"Now, here's my boss of two days lying on the floor. Do you know how long it took for me to find this job? Nobody is going to mess that up for me."

"Why would I. . ." A voice shouted for my attention, and I put the receiver back to my ear. "Yes, I'm still here. I won't hang up. Yes, she's still breathing—barely—but there's a lot of blood."

My cell phone rang. One glance showed the chief of police's number, my cousin Joe. Grimacing and offering apologies to the 911 operator, I answered it with my free hand. "I haven't touched anything."

"Uh-huh."

"Well, I did feel Mae Belle's neck to see if she was alive. She is. Oh, and I called from the office phone. Sorry. I didn't think to use my cell phone. I'm a little stressed right now. Plus, the desk was right there. Okay, so you know my fingerprints are on it. That shouldn't complicate things too much. Wait a minute. How did you know I was here?"

"April told me earlier that you had an

appointment. We heard the call come through. I put two and two together. Besides, you're drawn to trouble. We're on our way. Keep on not touching anything." *Click.*

Joe always was a man of few words. After slipping my cell phone back into my purse, I switched my attention back to dispatch. The woman droned on about CPR and how to staunch the blood flow.

Horror. "I'm not sure I should flip her on her back with something stuck there. Should I pull it out?" *Please say no.* The operator coaxed me on what to do, just in case, and to definitely not pull out the letter opener. My heart rate returned to normal. Sherry still stood nearby, as worthless as a chewed wad of gum.

"Get something to slow down the bleeding," I ordered.

Her eyes grew to the size of half dollars. "I don't do blood."

Good grief. Could I threaten to press charges for not assisting in trying to save someone's life? I glanced at my cousin. "Hang on, Mae Belle. You can't die. We've got a wedding to plan." Sirens wailed outside the building. "Help is here."

I hung up on the dispatch operator and leaned against the desk for support. During a crisis, I'm okay. Afterward, it all catches up to me. My skin grew clammy, my hands shook, and spots danced before my eyes. I watched the paramedics through tunnel vision.

"What's wrong with you?" Chief of police and man of compassion, Cousin Joe peered at me. "You aren't going to faint, are you? One semiconscious body is all we can handle at a time."

"I'm. . ." Peeking from beneath the desk pad was what appeared to be Mae Belle's appointment book. I turned to face Joe, hiding the desk behind my back.

I bet her attempted murderer was in that book. Amazing how the promise of another exciting mystery made me feel better. "I'm fine. Just woozy for a second. Thanks for being concerned."

"Right." He rushed off to do whatever it is he does and called over his shoulder, "don't go anywhere."

Sherry leaned against the wall, her eyes shooting daggers at me, as another officer took her statement. Her antagonistic attitude wore on me. *Death and destruction wherever I go?* That was just mean. When the officer finished with Miss Congeniality, he moved to me. "Name?"

"You know my name, Duane. We went to school together."

I crossed my arms. He raised his eyebrows at me.

"Fine. Summer Meadows."

"Business being here?"

"Planning a wedding." *Obvious, wasn't it?*

"You found the victim?"

"Yes." I quickly added that I didn't touch anything. Not being new to crime solving, I filled him in on everything I knew, except the date book. I'd turn it in once I had a chance to look through its pages. Joe would be livid, but he'd get over it. He'd been threatening for years to transfer to any town where *I* didn't live.

"So you were the last one to see Mae Belle before her attack?"

"No, the person who tried to kill her was." I didn't like the direction Duane's questions headed. What did Sherry mention to him? "Mae Belle acted nervous all morning. She wanted to tell me something, and we set up a time to meet at Grandma's Story Corner. Mae Belle never showed.

"I came to check on her, found her on the floor, and called 911. That's it. What did Sherry tell you?"

"What are you leaving out?" Duane peered at me from beneath his lowered brow.

"What do you mean?"

"Joe warned me about you withholding information."

"Not this time." I vowed to get even. How dare Joe accuse me of not telling him everything? The appointment book didn't count, did it? Since I couldn't be sure it even pertained to the morning's events.

"Uh-huh." Did the guy take lessons from my cousin in the disbelief department? He snapped his notebook closed. "We'll be in touch if we have any further questions. You aren't leaving town, are you?"

"Not until my honeymoon." They wouldn't prevent me from going, would they?

Bora Bora called my name, etching my new initials in its white sand. The sun sang its promises of sunburn. The waves chanted their rising and falling melodies. Remorse flooded through me.

Mae Belle may be dying, and I'm concerned

about getting married. Good thing no one could read my mind.

Paramedics wheeled her past me. Her eyelids fluttered as weak as a stunned moth. I prayed for her recovery. She wasn't strong. Tall and thin as the wildflowers that grew alongside Highway 64 in the spring. Okay, maybe she'd be stronger than she looked. Those wildflowers were almost impossible to kill. Especially when they took root among hopeful prize-winning rosebushes.

"Wait." I grabbed the stretcher and stopped it before bending low to whisper in Mae Belle's ear. "Don't worry. We'll find out who did this to you. I promise. You just get better so you can tell me." Releasing the rail, I stood and locked eyes with Joe.

"Summer, I'm warning you."

"What?" I did my best to appear as innocent as possible. The wide-eyed look always worked in the movies.

He marched to my side, grabbed my elbow, too roughly for my taste—I knew there'd be bruises—then pulled me into a corner. "You are *not* going to get involved in this. You are *not* the crime solver you think you are. You did *not* solve the past mysteries of this year with any skill. Stumbling onto them, and being lucky enough to remain alive, doesn't make you a detective. And I'm tired of saving your life."

"Sorry, Mr. Big Cop-Man, but I completely solved them on sheer brain power. And just because you're my cousin doesn't mean you can jerk me around. Ever hear of police brutality? It would be embarrassing for you if I filed a complaint, now wouldn't it?"

So what if I'd managed to get myself locked in a trunk. My double-jointedness saved me then. Being smart and keeping my cool got me out of the carnival fun house. What about the two gorillas? Or the overfriendly elephant, Ginger? Joe had no idea what he was talking about.

"Add tips from that stupid Dolt book you bought a few months ago, and you have the scope of your investigative training." Joe shook his head. "Summer, you just happen to be lucky. But luck runs out." He slapped his hat on his head. "Stay out of it, and leave this room. The crime scene investigators have a job to do."

"Let me get my bag, and I'll leave. "Once Joe turned his back, I snatched the appointment book off the desk, dropped it into the tote bag containing my wedding information, and sashayed out of A Dream Wedding with what I was sure was a Cheshire cat–type grin splitting my cheeks.

Miss Merry Sherry shooed Mae Belle's prospective customers from the sidewalk in front of the shop and handed a large, ornate brass key to a man in a navy vinyl jacket. With a final glare at me, she sidled sideways through the throng of investigators, slipped past the crime scene tape, then headed own Main Street.

I followed.

She passed my store, Summer Confections, and I waved through the window at Aunt Eunice. She threw her hands up as if to say, "What are you doing?"

I grinned and continued to slink along behind

my prey like a secret agent. Sherry turned to look over her shoulder. I ducked into an alley, ran straight into a Dumpster, grabbed my aching forehead, then landed smack on my behind in a puddle of oily water, ruining my new pair of studded blue jeans and twisting my ankle. This was definitely the norm for my crime solving.

Soaking wet and miserable,

3

Rising with all the grace of a fallen deer on an icy pond, I managed to get my feet beneath me. Grabbing my tote bag from the cement, goop leaving a nasty trail behind me, I limped to the corner and peered around the building.

Drat. No sign of Sherry. I absolutely could not go to the hospital and wait for news on Mae Belle while I resembled something that crawled out of a sewer drain. I'd go back to the candy store and let Aunt Eunice in on what happened before I'd head home to change clothes. She'd be angry if she heard the news from someone else.

Before stepping out onto the sidewalk, I noted the pedestrians. No one should be allowed to see me looking the way I did. I'd never live down the jokes and questions.

I turned to take the back way. The vacant alley loomed. My mind raced and clicked into detective mode.

Where had the attempted murderer run? Out the front door seemed doubtful. Not with the number of people milling in the receiving area and outside on the sidewalk.

Now I thought like a crime solver. First thought—had they tossed anything along the way?

After having practically tripped over it on my way to where I stood, the Dumpster behind A Dream Wedding beckoned like a box of jewels. Somebody who knew Mae Belle must have stabbed her. She'd never have gone into her office with a stranger. She was way too much of a Nervous Nellie. That same somebody had most likely ducked out the back door.

That's what I would have done. Maybe they tossed something in one of the trash receptacles. I scanned the length of the alley. Six beige Dumpsters lined up like square soldiers.

With a march as determined as an aching ankle and soggy denim pants would allow, I headed for the first one. This would be harder than I'd thought. The odor that emanated from beneath the hard plastic lid slapped me in the face with enough force to send me reeling back. My nostrils burned.

Gross. Okay, move on. No way would I climb in there. The next to the last one was almost empty. After piling milk crates on top of each other for the fifth time—and refusing to address the fact that the odor I held my breath against now actually came from me—I climbed and hung suspended over the edge.

Grunting from the pressure on my abdomen, I stretched to reach for a bag. A shrill siren whooped behind me. A camera clicked. I gasped and fell headfirst into black garbage bags and odd refuse. After pulling myself to my feet, I peeked over the top.

Horror. Joe stood, cell phone pointed at me, and snapped another picture.

"What are you doing?" I ducked until only my eyes peered over the rim.

He grinned. "Sending another picture to Ethan. He loves this stuff. He'll especially appreciate the one of your behind while you're Dumpster diving."

"Don't you dare!" I tried pulling myself over and out but ended up sliding back to the bottom.

"Too late." He frowned at me as I perched on top of garbage. "I think the question here is, what are you doing?"

"Uh, snooping?" I held out a hand for him to grasp. My foot slipped, and my gaze slid downward. At the bottom of my plastic prison lay a pair of black leather gloves. A telltale scarlet stain splattered across them. "Bingo!"

"Don't touch anything!"

I shrieked and clasped a hand to my chest. "There's no need to give me a heart attack."

"Come on. Get out of there. I'll have a team here in seconds."

"Why didn't they search the alley to begin with?"

"They're still inside. It doesn't take long for you to get in trouble." He helped me from the Dumpster. His eyes raked over me, and he wiped his hand down his pant leg. "Go home, clean up, and. . ."

"I know, stay out of it." I'm sure my family will engrave those words on my tombstone. I hobbled down the alley and banged on the back door of Summer Confections.

Aunt Eunice opened it. "What in the world

happened to you?" Before I could step inside and answer, Joe joined me. "Goodness. Both of you coming in the back like servants." Her disapproving tone washed over me as she moved aside.

Joe removed his hat and fiddled with the brim. "Aunt Eunice, I need to ask you something. Can we sit down?"

"Sure. There's a table in front." She wrinkled her nose. "Summer, you stink. What have you been doing?"

"Dumpster diving."

"Of all the things to be doing. Don't you have everything you need? No reason to dig in someone else's garbage." She waved a hand in my direction. "Stay behind the counter. We don't want the customers getting wind of you."

"I'm getting ready to go home and change." *As soon as Joe finishes talking to you.* I dug into my tote, pulled out a bottle of my favorite cologne, and liberally doused myself.

"Lord have mercy!" With a hand clamped over her nose, Aunt Eunice rushed through the swinging half-door that divided the customer area from our workplace. She and Joe sat at a small glass-topped table. My aunt folded her hands in front of her and waited. I leaned across the counter as far as possible without toppling over.

Joe gave one of his famous sighs. "No sense beating around the bush. Somebody in Mae Belle's store said they heard you threaten to kill her. Did you?"

Aunt Eunice was speechless—a rare moment in her life. Her mouth opened and closed like the gills on a fish. I thought she was beginning to cry, then realized her shoulders shook with silent laughter. How could she laugh at a time like this?

Oh, I hadn't had the chance to tell her about Mae Belle. She'd be overcome with remorse for her giggles. I started through the swinging door, caught a whiff of myself, and stopped.

"What did that girl tell you? Of course I didn't threaten to kill her. April made a joke and. . ."

"My April?" Joe's eyes widened.

"Do you know another girl with that name?" Aunt Eunice used the hem of her apron to wipe her eyes. "I started to say Mae Belle had better not mess up Summer's wedding, you know how she is. Then April asked if I was going to kill her if she did. It was all innocent, Joe. I assure you."

Joe leaned forward. "Someone sent Mae Belle to the hospital this afternoon with a letter opener sticking out of her back. Then I discover Summer digging through Dumpsters. Won't look good in an investigation, Eunice. The department will want me to be watching both of you."

I shrugged when she glanced my way. "I did discover some gloves through my searching. They aren't mine. You'll find that out when you do your tests. Then, Mr. Big Cop- Man, I'll be accepting your apology for even suggesting Aunt Eunice and I have anything to do with this." And I most likely ruined a pair of pants.

Joe's face reddened. "I never said I suspected. I didn't suggest. . ."

"Will Mae Belle be all right?" My aunt paled beneath the rosy blush she wore.

"I haven't made it over to check on her. Wanted to come by here first."

"Summer?" Aunt Eunice frowned so deeply her sparse brows came together in a line. "Why haven't you gone?"

"I was following Sherry, then I fell in a puddle of water and decided to check out the Dumpsters before coming here to tell you what happened."

Joe switched his attention to me. "Why were you following Sherry?"

"She was mean to me, and she didn't seem at all concerned that somebody tried to kill Mae Belle. Seemed more worried that she'd be out of a job. She actually insinuated I had something to do with it." I crossed my arms. "It made me suspicious."

"Mean to you?" Joe stood and shook his head. He had a habit of repeating what I said back in an annoying way.

One look at my watch and I rushed to the front door. "See y'all at the hospital. If I'm going to meet Ethan for dinner, I've got to change now." And I wanted a peek at Mae Belle's appointment book so bad I could almost taste the paper.

Sherry, my new nemesis, Joe, April, and Aunt Eunice sat in the hospital waiting room when I arrived. My sore ankle prevented me from wearing the strappy sandals I'd recently purchased. My flip-flops slapped against the tile. One of my aunt's pet peeves. "How is she? Did anyone call Uncle Roy? What about her parents in Oklahoma?" I collapsed into the nearest uncomfortable burgundy chair.

"The doctor hasn't come out." Aunt Eunice pulled a tissue from her brassiere and blew her nose, then glanced at my feet and scowled. "Roy will be here soon. He's closing the nursery early, and Mae Belle's parents have been notified. They'll be here in a few hours. How can I tell my sister I had ill thoughts of her daughter just moments before someone attacked her?"

I scooted from my seat and knelt in front of her. "You aren't the only one. . . ." A middle-aged man wearing a white lab coat approached us. Aunt Eunice gripped my hands until the knuckles ground together.

"I'm Dr. Barnett. Are you Miz Sweeney's family?" The doctor removed his glasses and rubbed the bridge of his nose.

"Yes." Joe stood, looking very much in control in his uniform. "How's Mae Belle?"

"I'm afraid there's nothing we could do. Miz Sweeney died on the table from internal bleeding caused by a small puncture to the heart. This is one time when extra weight on a person might have saved their life. I'm sorry." The doctor pinched the bridge of his nose again, nodded, and walked away.

Sherry wailed and buried her face in her hands. Most likely worrying about her next paycheck. I prayed for forgiveness for my awful thought. The Lord commands us to love our brother. How much more should I this woman? Or my cousin? And Mae Belle had died alone.

A lump rose in my throat, burning and making breathing difficult. Tears stung my eyes.

We sat in stunned silence. In the blink of an eye, we now looked at a murder case. Not for the death of a stranger, but for family.

4

Dusk fell, casting the early evening in the warm yellow glow of late summer. Remorse filled me as I dwelled on Mae Belle's death. I'd been so interested in gathering clues that I hadn't been by her side in the hospital. Granted, we weren't that close, not running in the same social circles, but I *had* hired her as a wedding planner. Against everyone's advice. But family is family. Personality didn't factor in, right?

Ethan slipped my shoes off my tired feet and massaged, gently cracking my toes. God really had sent me the best of the men He'd created. I snuggled deeper into the cushions of the porch swing and closed my eyes, losing myself in his touch.

"Are you going to be all right?" Ethan rubbed circles in the arch of my foot, his thumb pushing with the right amount of pressure. I bit back a moan.

"Yeah. April and Aunt Eunice will help me plan the wedding. We have eight months. They didn't want Mae Belle doing it anyway." My eyelids snapped open. "That sounded harsh, didn't it?

Especially with Mae Belle being murdered.

Sometimes I'm a horrible person." Ethan pulled me around until my back faced him. His strong fingers kneaded my tense shoulder muscles. He placed a soft kiss on the nape of my neck, and I thanked the Lord my aunt and uncle sat on the other side of the wall watching television. Experience taught me Ethan had a lot more willpower than I did.

"You're not a horrible person." He chuckled. "Joe sent me the most interesting picture on my phone today."

Uh-oh. Here it comes.

"Not that I didn't appreciate the view, but what were you doing hanging upside down in a Dumpster?" His fingers never paused in their massage. "Because, if I remember correctly, after the last escapade at the fair, a certain *someone* promised no more gumshoeing."

I didn't remember promising. *Horror.* A few months ago, I'd told God I'd tell no more white lies. There was no way out. I had to be honest. "But she's my cousin."

"I'm your fiancé. It's difficult to teach my students when I'm worried about you."

Great. A fist of guilt smashed me in the face. I turned to look at him. "I'm sorry. I won't put myself in harm's way. I'll just nose around a little. I have to do this, Ethan. As difficult as Mae Belle was, she didn't deserve to die that way. She was scared when she asked me to meet with her. Justice must be served." A worthy speech if I say so myself. "Besides, I promised."

"The last mystery you worked on, you said the same thing. Only that time, it had to do with your parents." Blue ice flashed from his eyes then disappeared under his solid resolve. Strong, gentle fingers brushed the hair away from my face. "Tinkerbell won't always be able to fly away."

His nickname used to fill me with anger when we were kids; now it caressed me with love. "You can help me again. Come with me when I ask questions."

"Who's on your suspect list this time?"

"No one. Yet."

"Then I'll pray you find out nothing and stay safe." He kissed me, sending bolts of electricity through my body. I thought, in a roundabout way, he'd given his permission. "I'll call you tomorrow."

He sauntered to his truck. With the rising moon casting him in silhouette, he raised a hand in farewell before driving away. I couldn't wait until he didn't have to leave at a decent hour. When I could, instead, grasp his hand and lead him into our home, our bedroom. This house.

Left to me by my parents. Eight more months. Then we'd be married, and my aunt and uncle moved into the new guesthouse being erected on a far corner of the land.

With a sigh, I rose to my feet and pulled open the squeaky screen door. Aunt Eunice turned her head from the game show on TV. "I wondered how long you were going to give the neighbors something to talk about. You know how people are in this small town." In her mind, I would perpetually be a teenager. "And would you tell me what all those letters piled on the floor of your closet mean?"

Case in point—I live with my aunt and uncle. I have no privacy. "Did you open them?"

She shook her head.

"Come upstairs, and I'll show you." Aunt Eunice bounded from her chair, patted my glued to-the-television uncle on the shoulder, then followed. Once inside my bedroom, I closed the door. A mound of envelopes in every shape, size, and color lay on the floor of my closet.

From beneath my bed, I pulled a plastic bag then dumped its contents. More envelopes spilled out. "I don't know what to do. I can't possibly answer them all." Especially since I'd been ignoring them for weeks.

"Who are they from?" Aunt Eunice picked up a pastel pink one.

"Fans. People asking for help." I plopped on the mattress sending letters fluttering to the floor. "They've been arriving at the candy store since I solved the murder at the carnival."

"You're famous." She ripped the envelope open. "This one is a proposal of marriage. You should show it to Ethan." She tossed it and opened another. "This one wants to hire you to find their missing dog. Maybe you've found a good source of a second income."

I went over to my nightstand and pulled a letter on navy-colored stationery from the drawer. "This one is a threat. I found it stuffed between the screen and the door when I came home today. Whoever sent it was unoriginal enough to cut letters from a newspaper or magazine."

Aunt Eunice's eyes widened as she read. "*Do not get involved. Is your life worth tracking down who killed a socially inept, abrasive personality of a woman?*" She flipped the page over. "*One who destroyed the dreams of those around her?*"

Her hand shook. "This person killed Mae Belle and has way too much free time. They must also know how nosy you are. Why else would they think you might try to solve your cousin's murder? You haven't been talking about it around town already, have you?"

"My thoughts exactly. And no, I haven't been talking. This person's prepared. We've only been home from the hospital for a few hours." I fell backward, sending more letters sliding to the floor. "How do I keep getting myself into these things?"

I groaned. "Ethan is going to kill me—or worse—cancel the wedding."

"Your uncle Roy will clean his guns again. In this last year, you've been the cause of him having the cleanest guns in Mountain Shadows." Aunt Eunice started scooping the papers into the bag. "Let's hide the evidence."

I scooted to the floor beside her. "What do I do with the rest of these? Toss them? Burn them?"

She shrugged. "We'll figure that out later. Maybe you can hire an assistant, being famous and all."

"Ha-ha. Look, I have something else." I pulled Mae Belle's appointment book from my tote. "I haven't had a chance to go through it yet, but I'm betting the name of Mae Belle's killer is in here."

"How did you get that?"

"I took it off her desk. When Joe told me to go away."

My aunt shook her head. "I'm not going to jail again, Summer. That was a very unpleasant experience."

"If I find anything, I'll turn it over to Joe. Until then, I'm taking notes. Then he can have the book." I flipped it open to this week's appointments. Most of the days had names scribbled across the page then crossed out. "

Wow. It'll take a lot of time to visit all these people."

Aunt Eunice peered over my shoulder. "It looks like she didn't do just weddings. I see a couple of parties." She ran her finger down the page. "Why are all the names scratched off ?"

"It's not like she was swimming in business. She left a long line of disgruntled customers. People who canceled." I snapped my fingers. "That's it. An unhappy patron killed her. We just have to find out who that person was. We can start with this list of crossed-off names. Somebody might know something they aren't aware they know."

"There's no 'we' to this, and don't jump to any conclusions. I promised your uncle Roy no more detective work. I'm a woman of my word." She leaned closer to me. "As you should be."

"Ethan gave me his permission tonight. Sort of." I slapped the book closed. "Tomorrow is Sunday. Some of these people will be at church."

"Don't forget we have to pick up Mae Belle's parents at the airport." Aunt Eunice groaned as she pushed to her feet. "It's been two years since I've seen my sister. I wish it was under different circumstances. No one should have to lose a child. How will I ever console Claudia?"

Aunt Claudia was difficult under the most pleasant of conditions. She made her daughter look like the nicest woman in Arkansas.

Sighing, I slid the notebook back into my tote, along with the threatening letter. Tomorrow promised to be a full day. I felt certain I would have a suspect by the time of the funeral.

5

Of course the pastor would choose this Sunday to speak on deceit. It amazed me how the sermons always seemed to fi t the situations in my life. No matter what I was

doing or dealing with, I'd find some nugget to take away with me. Sometimes not too flavorful of one.

I swished my straw in the watery whipped cream left in the bottom of my habitual Sunday frozen coffee. Anything to squelch the feelings that swirled like a dust devil in my conscience.

" 'Nor was any deceit in his mouth. . . .' "

My head jerked upright. What was the pastor saying? What did it mean? I glanced at the large screen hanging at the front of the sanctuary. Isaiah 53:9. I flipped through my Bible. The passage spoke of Christ's death. His innocence and love for us.

" 'Whoever would love life and see good days must keep his tongue from evil and his lips from deceitful speech.' "

Wait. The pastor went too fast. The pages of my Bible rippled as I tried to keep up while searching for 1 Peter 3:10. Keeping my tongue was about gossip, right? Not much of a problem there. But the words about deceitful speech lodged a lump in my throat the size of Pope County, Arkansas.

Murmuring words of apology, I squeezed past nearby parishioners, then yanked Joe from his seat. "I need to talk to you. Now." I tossed April a smile of apology.

With a roll of his eyes, Joe followed me to the annex. "What are you doing? You don't bolt out in the middle of a sermon." He crossed his arms. "This better be important. It isn't every Sunday I'm off work and able to take April to

church."

I squared my shoulders and pulled the appointment book from my tote. "I found this in Mae Belle's office." I held it out to him and breathed a sigh of release when he took it. "I wasn't honest with you yesterday. There may be a clue inside as to who killed her."

Joe chewed the inside of his cheek before answering. "You actually listened to the pastor's words?"

Of all the nerve. "I always listen." *I just don't always hear.*

"Uh-huh." He flipped through the pages. "I guess I don't need to ask whether you've already looked at it."

Looked and memorized the names. "Of course I did. Do you want it or not?"

"Yes." He raised his gaze to mine. "What did you plan on doing with these names?"

"Same as you. I'm going to question everyone

in there. I'll share any information I uncover with you."

"Uh-huh."

"Stop saying that. You need to work on your vocabulary. Also, I've received a lot of mail from folks wanting me to help them solve their own little mysteries. Yesterday, I received this." I handed him the threatening note and waited for him to read the pasted-on words.

His brows drew together. "This isn't funny, Summer."

"I didn't say it was. It's frightening, actually." The lump in my throat dissipated. Amazing what clearing your conscience did for a person. Now all I needed to do was come clean with Ethan. "I promise not to keep anything else from you. Will you do the same?"

"I'm a police officer. I can't share details of a crime with you."

"Is there anything in the law that says I can't visit with the people on that list?"

"Visit, no. Interfere with—"

The church service released, and we were immediately swarmed by people. Hugs for me, handshakes for Joe, and condolences for both of us in regard to Mae Belle's death.

Within minutes we were parted as effectively as Moses parted the Red Sea. Ethan swept through the throng and whisked me outside. I tossed my empty coffee cup in the nearest trash bin.

"There's no time for socializing. Not if we're going to get to the airport on time." He led me to my car, situated me in the passenger seat, then loped to the driver's side. "Sorry to yank you away, but we're in danger of being late."

"No problem." He'd only saved me from a lecture I preferred not to hear. I put on my seat belt. It'd be better to tell him of my falsehood while he drove. He wouldn't be able to get too upset. In true Summer fashion, once I decided on an action, I spilled my guts and vomited out everything from taking the book to receiving the note.

Ethan's jaw clenched as he kept his eyes on the road. "Why do you insist on not being truthful with me?"

"It's not that I'm lying, just withholding information."

"Same thing." For the next thirty minutes the silence in the car screamed, banging against my eardrums. My gaze kept flickering to Ethan's clenched jaw. His anger didn't bother me, much. It never lasted long. The fact he was disappointed in me, did.

Finally, Ethan pulled my hand from my lap and tightened his fingers around mine. "I love you, Summer. I can't keep you safe if you keep things from me."

"I'm working on it, Ethan. I am. The note wasn't put on our porch until late afternoon."

"You could have called me." He spared me a glance.

"What could you have done?" I rubbed his calloused palm with my thumb.

He shrugged and focused back on the road ahead of us. "You didn't give me the chance to do anything. Not come over and reassure you—

nothing."

"I'm sorry."

"What are the names in Mae Belle's book? Maybe I can shed some light on this for you."

Ethan had to be the most wonderful man in the world. Gnawing my bottom lip, I forced my memory to remember the names. "Hubert Smith."

"The dentist? Makes sense. He was engaged to Edna Mobley, but they canceled."

Hence the marks through their names. "Renee Richards."

"The Princess of Mountain Shadows? What would she want with Mae Belle? Her fiancé is in Iraq.

"Mason White."

Ethan frowned. "I've heard the name but don't think I know him. Wait. Yes, I do. A playboy. Was a grade behind me in high school. Who else?"

"Larry Bell."

"Why would a farmer need Mae Belle's services? Anyone else?" I shook my head.

"Quite a motley list and not very big."

"All the names were scratched out. Like cancellations."

The airport came into view, and I glanced at my watch. "The plane lands in ten minutes. We made it."

The security at Little Rock National Airport being what it was, we opted to wait for Mae Belle's parents next to the baggage claim. Voices rose and fell as suitcases tumbled onto the carousel to be snatched up by waiting hands. Hugs were passed around like cookies at Christmas. I smiled at the joyous reunions.

Finally, Claudia Sweeney approached, shuffling her feet. A woman as large as Mae Belle had been skinny. Beside her, a firm grip on her elbow, ambled my Uncle Fred, who resembled a praying mantis, minus the green.

Aunt Claudia lumbered up to me. Her glare could have burned through steel. "Summer Meadows, what are you doing to find the man who did this to my baby girl? Don't say you ain't doing nothing. You meddle in everyone else's business. Now you got to take care of your own."

"Uh." I shrank back. "We don't know that it was a man."

"Don't mince words with me. What are you planning to do?"

"The police are handling things."

She raised her arm. I thought for a moment she would strike me. The woman's face fell. She covered her head with her hands and wailed. Then she tossed her arms over her head. Her fists clutched the tight gray curls spiraled on top of her head.

Help me out, Lord. I laid a trembling hand on her arm, not sure how to handle someone else's hysterics, despite having shown plenty of my own during my life.

Ethan deserted me with a sheepish look and took Uncle Fred to collect the luggage. I'd deal with him later.

Aunt Claudia lifted red-rimmed eyes to mine. "By police, you mean my nephew, Joe." She shook her head. "He's the definition of a bumbling country boy if I ever saw one. You'll have to do this for me, Summer."

"I'll do my best, Aunt Claudia. But give Joe some credit. He's done just fine as our chief of police."

That didn't satisfy my aunt, who kept after me until I vowed. Whatever it took, I'd find Mae Belle's killer.

Aunt Claudia clasped me to her massive bosom, threatening to suffocate me within her mounds of flesh. "You are the sweetest thing. I'll help you however I can. Now let's go and see my sister."

To accommodate Aunt Claudia's bulk, we had her sit up front, with the seat as far back as it would go. Uncle Fred folded himself in behind Ethan, and I hugged my knees for the hour drive home.

After Ethan pulled between Aunt Eunice's and Uncle Roy's matching 1962 Chevy pickups, I breathed a sigh of relief and toppled out of the car. My legs had fallen asleep.

Aunt Claudia shook her head. "Get up, girl. We have work to do."

"Are you all right?" Ethan rushed to my side and helped me to my feet.

"I can't feel my legs."

He chuckled and swung me into his arms. His long strides carried us past my relatives, and he deposited me on the porch swing. "I'll be back after I help your uncle with the suitcases."

I enjoyed the view as he marched away then marveled as his muscles bunched beneath the royal blue polo shirt he wore as he hefted the luggage. Did he feel the same when he watched me? Petite, thin, with a head of red hair I dyed brown and called auburn? I sighed and rubbed the prickly feeling from my tingling legs. Definitely, God hadn't spared any decoration when creating Ethan.

"Claudia!" Aunt Eunice barged through the screen door and wrapped her plump arms halfway around her sister.

Aunt Claudia abruptly burst into a loud wail in the middle of the driveway.

"Oh, you poor thing." Aunt Eunice kept an arm around the distraught woman and led her into the house. *Thank You, Lord, that I didn't have to comfort her.* That was a characteristic God left out of my DNA.

Legs back to normal, I pushed my foot against the wood floor of the porch and set the swing into action. How was I going to solve Mae Belle's murder with the albatross of Aunt Claudia hanging around my neck?

Conviction pummeled me. I wanted to be more compassionate. I did. I prayed for just an ounce. Enough to help me get Aunt Claudia through the loss of her only child.

I straightened my shoulders. I could solve my cousin's murder *and* be a shoulder to cry on for my aunt. Hopefully, I'd survive both.

6

Sleep drifted in like mist over a lake, sneaking among my tossing and turning on the sofa. Aunt Claudia and Uncle Fred had gushed their thanks earlier when I offered them my bed. Made me really wish I'd fixed up the spare room for guests instead of using it as a place to store everything that had no home. Sleeping on the couch could be dangerous. At least for me. I tended to roll off .

The bickering of sibling voices woke me. Soft rays of light sifted through the partially open curtains. I groaned, pushed my cairn terrier, Truly, off my stomach, and pulled the pillow over my head. Even that didn't drown out the voices coming from the kitchen.

"She has a book. With Mae Belle's appointments."

"I want to see it."

"Settle down, Claudia. I've got her tote bag right here. What do you plan on doing with the names?"

"Hunt down my baby's killer."

They're going through my bag? I tossed the

pillow to the floor and bolted upright.

"It ain't here. She must have moved it."

"What is all that stuff?"

"Wedding notes, Claudia." Papers rustled, and I threw off my blankets. They were going to get everything unorganized.

"Only a harlot would wear a wedding dress with no shoulders in it." Aunt Claudia's voice cut through the walls to my buzzing ears. "Pure and demure. That's what a bride should be. Is this a shotgun wedding?"

Heat spread up my neck and set my cheeks on fire.

"Of course not! Give me that picture."

"And what kind of a cake is this? That is not a traditional bride and groom on top. Why, they're in an embrace! It's shocking."

"It's Summer's wedding. She can have what she wants."

My heart warmed at Aunt Eunice's defense. I slipped my feet into fuzzy teddy bear slippers, scratched Truly behind the ears, then padded my way to the kitchen. Aunt Eunice held a picture of my wedding gown.

Aunt Claudia buried her face in her arms and sobbed. "My baby will never have a wedding. She had men standing in line to date her, you know."

"I know how upset you are, Claudia. I've lost loved ones, and I'm praying for you." Aunt Eunice slipped an arm around her sister. "Did you and Mae Belle resolve your differences?"

"No." The crying stopped when Aunt Claudia spotted me in the doorway. "She still couldn't finish anything she ever started. Now Summer, where's the book with the names?"

"I gave it to Joe. It might be evidence." I made a beeline for the coffeepot. No way could I handle these two without a huge dose of caffeine. After filling my mug with the fragrant brew, I turned and stared at the sisters. "We have an appointment at the funeral home in an hour, and I don't appreciate you going through my things."

That started the wailing again. For the first time, I got a look at Aunt Claudia's face during a crying jag. No tears. No bloodshot eyes. My investigative antennae went straight up. Our gazes locked. She dropped her head on folded arms and sniffled.

What a fake! Now to find out why the

Academy Award–winning act.

"There's no money for a funeral." Aunt Claudia grabbed a napkin and dabbed her dry eyes. She peered at her sister from beneath lowered lashes. "Me and Fred have fallen on hard times."

"Oh sweetie, don't you worry about a thing. We've got money, don't we, Summer?"

Where did *we* have that kind of money? My savings? My aunt's cruise fund? "Sure. We'll help." I buried my face in my mug.

"You two are such dears." Aunt Claudia pushed her bulk out of the chair and got to her feet. She leaned against the table for support. "I'll go upstairs and find something to wear."

Once I heard her lumber to her room, I turned to Aunt Eunice. "You have *got* to be kidding. I don't have that kind

of cash." My aunt sent me a pleading look. I

sighed. "I'll use my charge card." It was family after all.

A grin split her face. "You pay half, and I'll pay the rest." Aunt Eunice clasped me to her ample flannel-covered bosom.

I disentangled myself. "I'd better get dressed."

When my parents died a month before I turned six, I'd worn a pink ruffled dress to the funeral home. The one my dad said made me look like his little princess. As an adult, I didn't think it would be appropriate to wear something frilly, and I flipped through the clothes hanging in my closet.

What did one wear to pick out a coffin? In Mountain Shadows, the viewing and funeral would warrant wearing a dress. I might as well be comfortable today. I chose black pants and a maroon blouse.

"Well, Truly, girl." I spoke to my cairn terrier through the clothing as I tugged it over my head. "Something is rotten in Denmark or, in this case, the Meadows home." My head free at last, I stepped into the pants. "Aunt Claudia acts the part of a grieving parent, but my gut tells me she's nothing but a big old fraud." Truly barked what I took to be agreement.

"The question is"—I tugged the skinny pants over my hips—"why? I don't mind forking over the cash for the funeral, well not completely anyway, but something doesn't make any sense. And what do you want to bet Aunt Claudia picks the most expensive coffin?"

Mountain Shadows Funeral Home had been built to look like a Southern plantation complete with carved white pillars on a wrap-around porch. Magnolia trees graced the sweeping lawn behind a driveway that circled a stone fountain. Definitely the place to be prepared for burial.

I still hadn't gotten over what Aunt Claudia had decided to wear. I could barely keep my eyes off the back of her fuchsia-colored, yellow flower-patterned muumuu. Fluorescent yellow flip-flops slapped against the brick path.

Aunt Eunice elbowed me. "Stop staring. Claudia thinks she looks nice. She doesn't have much money, you know."

Or fashion sense. I checked my tote bag to make sure the names I'd written in a new notebook still nestled in the bottom. A person never knows when they might stumble upon a clue. And every one of my crime-solving books suggests a detective be prepared for anything.

A heavily made-up woman with teased hair greeted us in a soft, comforting voice when we entered through the double-glass doors. She motioned us into a room to choose a coffin, and Aunt Claudia immediately ran her hand over the polished woods and stainless steel surfaces.

She oohed and aahed and finally motioned to her choice. I peeked at the price tag. The Spring Rose. Moss pink, velvet interior. Price tag, three thousand, four hundred and fifty dollars! I gulped, then reassured myself it could have been worse. I had to admit it was beautiful.

When I die, just fry me. Save the money for something that won't be stuffed into the ground.

We exited the showroom and entered a plush

office in green velvet and brass. The three of us squeezed onto the sofa, with me sandwiched in the middle. I was wedged in so tight if someone yelled fire, I was a goner.

A thin man, complete with a pencil mustache, peered at us over his steepled fingers. The nameplate on his desk identified him as Lewis Anderson.

He placed a pair of gold-rimmed reading glasses on his nose and curled his hand around a silver ballpoint pen. "I'm sorry for your loss." His deep voice rumbled through the room. "I have a few questions for you, then I'll handle the rest."

We nodded in unison. Aunt Claudia blurted, "We've chosen the Something-Rose casket."

Mr. Anderson raised his eyebrows. "The Spring Rose? Excellent choice." He made a note. "Religious preference?"

"Christian, of course. There ain't no way my daughter is going to partake in any heathen ceremony."

"Ah, the mother." He scribbled something else. "Burial, selected plot out back, pastor of attending church will preside?" He widened his eyes. "Am I being too presumptuous?"

We shook our heads again. I gnawed my lower lip. Something about this guy bothered me. What did he mean by a selected plot?

"Have the authorities released the body?"

A sheen appeared in his dark eyes. Were those tears?

I shifted my weight, trying to squeeze from my prison. "Not yet. Possibly tomorrow."

"All right then." He flipped through his calendar. "We could do the viewing on Wednesday. That gives the medical examiner an extra day, and the funeral service can be held on Thursday. I'm assuming you want a traditional service?"

"Of course we do!" Aunt Claudia rose, almost taking me with her. "Nothing is too good for my Mae Belle."

Mr. Anderson gave a thin smile and blinked his eyes. He definitely appeared to be struggling not to cry. I detected a faint quiver to his chin.

He handed Aunt Claudia a sheet of paper. "This is what's included in our traditional service. Mountain Shadows Funeral Home is honored to help you during this difficult time."

Aunt Claudia handed the paper to me without glancing at it. My stomach churned as my gaze rolled down the page. Moving the body to the funeral home. Cosmetology. Dressing the body. Pallbearers. The final line almost stopped my heart. Nine thousand dollars, including the casket. *Catch me, Lord. I'm going to faint.*

"Ladies, have a wonderful day." The man actually grasped my aunts by their elbows and steered them through the door. He turned to me.

I stopped. "Mr. Anderson, how well did you know Mae Belle?"

"Excuse me?"

"You seem overly affected by her death and the funeral arrangements. Are you this personable with all your customers?"

He straightened his shoulders and shifted his eyes. "I'm afraid I didn't have the honor of making her acquaintance."

If I've learned anything from reading my crime books, it's that a liar often glances over the questioning person's left shoulder. Just like he did. What could Mr. Anderson have to hide?

7

Soft music filled the quiet atmosphere in the viewing room. Mae Belle, wearing more makeup than I'd ever seen her wear, lay in the casket with hands folded across her stomach. We'd been sitting there for an hour before the first visitor arrived.

Sherry marched through the door and strode to stare down at Mae Belle. The former secretary of A Dream Wedding took a deep breath and said something I couldn't hear. Her lips thinned into a tight smile, she whirled, glowered at me, then marched back out.

What did the woman have against me? I didn't remember ever having met her before hiring Mae Belle. Had I wronged her as a kid?

Over the course of the two-hour viewing, less than ten people, spaced sporadically, arrived to pay their respects. Boredom overtook me. I picked at my cuticles and wished Ethan hadn't been too busy to come with me. My aunts huddled in the first row of chairs and whispered together.

Occasionally, Aunt Claudia's wails drowned out the music. Forgive me, Lord, but I'd had enough. I dashed outside to the parking lot where my uncles hid out beneath one of the magnolia trees. Smart men. I made my way over to them.

"Mae Belle looked beautiful, didn't she?"

Uncle Fred wiped his sleeve across his eyes. "Yes, she did. Not much of a turnout, but my little girl had trouble making friends. Too much like her ma."

I must have looked shocked because Uncle Fred shrugged and clapped me on the shoulder. "Don't worry. I might keep my mouth shut around the women in my life, but I'm not deaf or dumb. You just find out who killed her, okay?"

I nodded.

Thursday morning, Aunt Claudia thumped down the stairs wearing a black muumuu with pink flowers and silver flip flops. I smoothed a hand down my own black dress, shook my head, and turned away to avoid her seeing my expression.

Uncle Fred wore an outdated-looking but fitted gray suit, and Uncle Roy looked dapper in a navy one. Aunt Eunice appeared behind her sister, wearing a full black skirt and gray blouse. The only similarity between the two, other than their body shape, was the shape of their noses and the gray curls on their heads.

Aunt Eunice's red-rimmed eyes, as befitted the day of grieving, met my gaze over her sister's head. Aunt Claudia's eyes were suspiciously bright and dry. They didn't appear to be suffering from any lack of sleep.

I'd written her name at the top of my suspect list the evening before. It would have been impossible for her to make it here from Oklahoma and get home again before we called to tell her about Mae Belle, but I'd bet the candy store the woman was involved somehow.

We stepped out of the house into sunshine. The uncles escorted the aunts into my car, and I sat on the porch swing to wait for Ethan. I'd chosen not to squeeze in the back seat with the other women. Not after yesterday's squashing experience. And Mr. Anderson became my number-two suspect after that meeting.

A warm rush of confidence washed over me. Less than a week and I already had two suspects. This mystery should be wrapped up and tossed away before another seven days passed. My eyes would be open and peeled at the funeral this afternoon. In the movies, the killer always showed up to view the results of the evil deed.

Ethan's truck rolled into the driveway, and I bounded from my seat. He looked gorgeous. The royal blue of his shirt set off his azure eyes and golden curls. The slow, sweet smile he gave me as I slid in beside him sent a flush of heat up my neck.

"Good morning, beautiful." He reached over and squeezed my hand.

"Morning, Ethan." If he didn't stop looking at me with those smoldering eyes, we'd never make it to church. That reminded me of another fee I'd have to pay. Transportation back and forth from the funeral home. I sighed.

"What's the matter, Tink?" Ethan's large hand engulfed mine.

"I offered to pay half of Mae Belle's funeral. I

don't regret helping. It's just that Aunt Claudia spared no expense, and I've got the feeling her grief is all an act." I proceeded to fill him in on her tearless sobbing.

"Have you mentioned your suspicions to Joe?"

"Of course not. He thinks I'm a doofus. Aunt Claudia is staying in our house—for way longer than we'd like. I'll get to the bottom of this." Ditching the woman when I was investigating Mae Belle's death would probably be the biggest challenge.

We arrived at church before the aunts and uncles exited my car. Ethan pulled into an empty space beside them. I glanced around the parking lot. Not a crowd. Less than twenty cars. Sadness engulfed me. Mae Belle's sandpaper personality turned off many people. Today it showed.

"There's a few of the names on your list here." Ethan motioned toward the attendees milling in front of the building. "That little woman is Edna Mobley."

Edna looked as if a strong wind could pick her up and move her fifty yards down the road. She'd pulled mousy hair streaked with gray into a tight bun at the nape of her neck. A serviceable brown suit completed the stereotype of a librarian.

Ethan continued talking as we slid from the truck. "That man staring at her is Hubert Smith, Edna's former fiancé and the local dentist. Edna works for him."

The man reminded me a bit of Mr. Toad. Skinny legs, round belly, balding head, and wire-rimmed spectacles that slid down a flat nose. Ethan grasped my elbow and steered me toward the doors as he continued his commentary. "You've met Lewis Anderson. The man he's speaking with is Larry Bell."

Bell shuffled a sneakered foot in the gravel while listening to whatever it was Anderson had to tell him. Bell shrugged and disappeared into the small crowd, his plain gray slacks and shirt blending in with the surroundings.

It seemed considerate that Mae Belle's disgruntled clients would come to the service. I hated to think of how small the crowd would have been had they not. I searched for the other two names on the list.

One face I'd recognize if I saw her. Renee Richards. The head cheerleader and homecoming queen of my senior year. It had grated on my nerves to stand beside her as one of her ladies-in-waiting. I'd drooled over that crown for two years. No sign of the former queen.

Sherry, the "I don't do blood" lady, sat on a marble bench, a cigarette clenched between her fingers. Her hunched shoulders showed she carried more burden than Mae Belle's own mother.

Anderson announced it would be time to start in a couple of minutes, and the not-so-large crowd shuffled inside and filled the first two rows of the funeral room. I sat between the Meadows relatives and the Sweeneys in the front middle section of seats.

Mae Belle's lovely bronze casket graced the floor in front. From my seat, the only part of her I could see was her nose, rising above the pink velvet interior like a smokestack.

Aunt Claudia fidgeted in her seat, glancing over her shoulder. "Ain't many people here, is there? That's what happens when you have a funeral in the middle of the day. Otherwise, this place would be packed. Nothing draws the curious like a funeral of someone murdered. Which of them do you think killed her?"

My gaze scanned the group. Not a likely looking murderer in the bunch. Joe rushed in and took a seat in the back. He met my gaze and shook his head as if to signal me not to let on he was there. Did he think the same thing I'd thought earlier? That Mae Belle's killer would be here?

Aunt Eunice elbowed me, eliciting a grunt, and forced me to turn around. Maybe I could study people more at the grave site.

The pastor spoke of how Mae Belle came from humble beginnings to business owner. He went on to speak of how much the only child was loved by her parents. Then he shot my idea out of the sky. Graveside services were for immediate family only. Now why would Aunt Claudia agree to that?

She seemed to seek attention. Her wails threatened to drown out the pastor's words. I flashed Aunt Eunice a look. She shrugged.

Service completed, everyone stood and filed past the casket. I paused and laid a hand on Mae Belle's hard cold one. The cosmetologist had made her look almost pretty— different, but pretty. Again, I promised to find her killer and blinked away tears of remorse. If I'd thought to check on her earlier, I might have spared her this. Instead, I'd chosen to finish my coffee and give her time to show up at the bookstore.

Once through the line, I made a beeline to Joe. "Who do you think it is?"

"What?" His gaze flicked to mine then back to the crowd.

"The killer. Isn't that why you're here? Because you think he is?" I tried to determine where he looked.

"I can't discuss that with you. I'm here because Mae Belle was my cousin."

"Then I won't tell you what I've discovered." I folded my arms.

"You can't withhold information, Summer."

"Humph." I marched away. There was no new information, and I knew he wouldn't believe my suspicions about our aunt. I'd just have to investigate her myself.

Ethan and I drove two car lengths behind the hearse. The early autumn foliage rolled past the slow-moving vehicles in a kaleidoscope of olive and forest green while the sun's rays shot dapples through the colorful tree branches.

Mountain Shadows Cemetery waited just outside town. Four cars pulled to a stop. Ethan, Joe, Uncle Fred, Uncle Roy, and two men I didn't know hefted the casket from the back of the hearse and carried it to the grave site.

Aunt Eunice sniffled background music to her sister's sobs. As the casket was lowered into its new home, the back of my neck prickled.

Maybe it was the chill of a breeze promising winter. Or maybe the scent of dried leaves already on the ground. But something disturbed the peace of the moment.

I glanced over my shoulder. The silhouette of a man, or possibly a tall woman, stood in the shadows of a magnolia tree staring toward our small family cluster.

8

The cherries I dipped in the sugar coating lined the tray like round boulders lining a driveway. I grasped the first one by its stem and swirled it through the dipping machine. The loveliest shade of dark chocolate fell in rivulets from the fruit to join the rest in the tempering pan.

If only mysteries were solved as efficiently. Covered as easily as cherries with chocolate. I sighed and allowed my mind to focus on my list of suspects as my hand performed the task I could probably do in my sleep.

Who should I visit first? One of the two who had not attended Mae Belle's funeral? I shook my head.

Renee Richards would not be a pleasant visit. She'd be all sugar acting on the outside and acid corroding with her sweet words on the inside. Made me want to gag.

I also wasn't comfortable visiting Mountain Shadows' playboy, Mason White. Not alone anyway. Aunt Eunice already warned me about the type of man Mason was. Maybe she could get away from her sister long enough to go with me.

The two of them bickered behind the counter. Aunt Claudia insisted on helping pack boxes of assorted chocolates but ate more than she packed. Or else skimped on the candy, leaving the boxes at less than their intended weight.

My customers were used to a certain standard of service. We'd hear from them if things weren't up to par.

"Just because you're the oldest dooon't mean you can boss me around." Aunt Claudia yanked a box from Aunt Eunice's hands.

"It's my store. That makes me the boss of anyone working here." Aunt Eunice snatched the box back.

I raised my eyes at her comment. Actually, I was the boss, considering I owned the place. I'd better go referee what threatened to become a full-scale sibling war.

"Shouldn't one of the perks of working in a candy store be sampling the merchandise?" Aunt Claudia plopped on a stool.

"Yes, but you've eaten at least ten pieces, and you don't technically work here!"

I removed the box from Aunt Eunice's clenched fists hoping the chocolates inside weren't smashed. "Aunt Claudia, we'll give you this box to take home with you. We don't expect you to work while you're grieving. I'll call Uncle Roy to come and get you."

She stomped her foot. "Don't bother. Seeing as how you're more interested in making candy than finding out who murdered my baby, I think I'll hit the pavement. Might scare up some information.

You can just bring the stuff home with you."

She'd scare up something, all right. However, I doubted it would be clues. She marched out of the store, still wearing one of my red-ruffled aprons over her yellow and green muumuu. With her curls beneath a hairnet, she made a strange picture as she clomped down the sidewalk.

I watched until she disappeared into the diner. "Will she be all right?" I closed the door behind her.

Aunt Eunice waved a hand. "She'll be fine. Maybe she can work off some of that orneriness." She took the stool her sister had vacated. "Summer, I need to talk to you."

"Let me turn off the dipping machine. There's something I want to talk to you about, too." I slid the dipped cherries in front of the fan and clicked off the machine before pulling a stool opposite my aunt.

"Have you noticed anything odd about Claudia?" Aunt Eunice propped her chin in her hand.

"Like a lack of mourning for her daughter? Or at least *real* mourning. Yes, I have." *Please don't yell at me. But you did bring up the subject.*

"What do you make of it? When your parents died, I cried all the time. That was for a nephew. Not my own child. I thought my sister would be a wreck."

My shoulders slumped. "I'm not sure. She didn't kill Mae Belle. Oklahoma may be next door to Arkansas, but it's still a three-hour drive. You said the two were estranged. Why?"

"It's stupid, really. Mae Belle wouldn't move

back home and marry the neighbor boy. Claudia feared she was seeing someone here, but the girl wouldn't say who." Aunt Eunice raised her eyes to mine. "I think my sister is up to something, and it ain't good. Could Mae Belle have had money we don't know about?"

I popped a chocolate cream into my mouth and allowed the flavor to melt with a heavenly rich taste before answering. "I don't think so. She didn't appear like a flamboyant person. Now, don't get mad at me, but Aunt Claudia is on my suspect list."

A look of resignation came over her face. She was undoubtedly remembering the other time I'd listed her best friends as my number ones. "Who else?"

The names from Mae Belle's appointment book rattled across my tongue with the speed of a machine gun. I watched the expressions flitter across my aunt's face.

Her brows furrowed. "Think there's anything to the names being crossed off?" I asked.

"Yeah." She rose. "They most likely canceled their appointments. Not many people around here had faith in Mae Belle's ability to run anything efficiently. That girl was a walking disaster."

"You don't think one of them might have killed her?"

Where would I start if not with this list? "Just a guess, but one of them most likely did. Why don't you start with Mason White?"

"Why him?"

" 'Cause he's walking through the door." I swirled on my stool and came face-to-face with the handsome, charming Mason White.

If I didn't love my husband-to-be so strongly and had already deemed him the most handsome man on earth, I would have given pause to appreciate Mason's gifts to women. Hazel eyes sparkled like jewels, thick brown hair swept back from a strong forehead, and a dimple in his chin could pool water.

He grinned and leaned across the counter with dentist-whitened teeth. "Ladies."

"Mr. White." Aunt Eunice stepped to the counter. "What can we get for you?"

"A three-pound box of your finest."

Aunt Eunice frowned at me over her shoulder and mouthed for me to get over there. *Horror!* What would I ask the guy first? I couldn't just blurt out that I'd seen his name in a dead woman's appointment book.

"Why'd you cancel your appointment with Mae Belle?"

His smile faded. "Excuse me?"

Aunt Eunice rolled her eyes as she passed to get the assortment and whispered, "and you call yourself a detective. Real subtle."

"I managed to get a glimpse of Mae Belle's appointment book before the police confiscated it. Your name was crossed out."

The man chucked me under the chin. "Aren't you the cutest thing? I'd heard you fancied yourself a pseudo-detective

of sorts. Rest your pretty little self, Summer. I canceled an arrangement I had with the poor woman. Nothing more."

I narrowed my eyes. "What kind of an arrangement?"

"A dinner party. One of those mystery-murder game nights. Just a small group of friends for a night of revelry. The prude refused to factor in alcohol. She obviously didn't believe in the saying that the customer is always right."

His eyes roamed over me. "But a looker like you probably knows how to have fun, am I right?"

Puhleese! He made me want to shower as soon as I got home. "Did you visit her shop on Friday?"

Aunt Eunice handed him the box and took his money.

"Now why would I do that after canceling? You don't think *I* killed the woman, do you?" He burst into laughter. "Priceless. You are absolutely priceless. I've been known to get into a bit of trouble now and then, but murder? I don't think so. And you were such a quiet little thing in high school."

Now I remembered him. I must have chosen to block out his arrogant swagger down the high school halls. Completely unconvinced of his innocence, I locked gazes with him and gnawed at my lower lip. The man was incorrigible.

I was tempted to move him to the top of my list simply for being a slimeball. "Can we get you anything else?" I folded my arms.

"This is it."

I backed up to take my seat on the stool. It rolled from beneath me, landing me hard on my bottom on the cold tile floor. The breath left me with a grunt. Face burning, I scrambled to my feet and sat with as much dignity as I could muster after sprawling on the floor.

Mason stopped at the door and turned, his face without expression. He grinned again. "You be careful, little girl. I heard your cousin got it in the back when she wasn't looking."

Aunt Eunice gasped.

9

He warned me, Ethan. And not in the friendly way of being concerned for my welfare."

The night chill had sent us inside, and we snuggled on the sofa in front of the television. Uncle Roy stared unblinking at some extreme sports show on cable television.

"Mae Belle did get it in the back. It was probably Mason's idea of a joke." Ethan squeezed my hand.

"He didn't look like he was joking." I entwined my fingers with his, enjoying how his big hand engulfed my smaller one.

"Do you want me to talk to him?" Ethan smoothed the hair from my face.

"Goodness, no. That'll make me look scared."

"You are scared."

"Who is?" Uncle Roy tore his attention from the television.

"Somebody threatening you, Summer?" He moved to rise from his chair. "I'll go get my gun."

"There's no need for your gun, Uncle Roy." He thought that answered everything. I'm surprised Joe hadn't relieved him of it.

Aunt Claudia entered the room and squeezed into the armchair next to Uncle Roy's recliner. She kicked off her flip-flops and used her hands to lift her feet to the coffee table. "Boy, howdy! Nancy Drew, I ain't. My dogs are killing

me. I don't know how you do it, Summer."

I don't walk aimlessly around town for one thing. If I'm pounding the pavement, I've got a purpose. "I didn't find out much either."

"Did you leave that store of yours?"

"No, but. . ."

"Well, there's your problem. How are you going to solve anything stuck between four walls? Do you think that worthless cousin of yours has taken the tape off Mae Belle's place of business? I'd like to get in there. And what about her apartment? Are the police still searching it? Can we check that out tomorrow and take anything of value? You don't work on Saturday, do you?"

The woman's mouth ran like white water. You could almost raft on her words.

I interrupted. "I thought I would since I've missed so many days this—"

"Perfect." She struggled to her feet. "I'm hitting the sack. See you in the morning. Wear something scroungy, and we'll pack up my daughter's apartment. Best way to find something. Get rid of everything, piece by piece."

Nothing like letting Mae Belle's body cool. Aunt Claudia was definitely searching for something, and I intended to find out what.

Aunt Eunice stood in the doorway, a look of incredulity on her face. We sat in silence until we heard the thump of Aunt

Claudia's feet upstairs. Aunt Eunice plopped into the chair her sister had vacated. "Well, she obviously thinks Mae Belle left something behind. Roy, do you think you could get information out of Fred?"

He shrugged. "I don't even know what to ask the guy. He doesn't say much. Talks in grunts. He spoke more to Summer at the viewing than I've ever heard him say."

"Well, see if he can't grunt what his wife's looking for. He's in the kitchen making a sandwich. Go on and ask him." Aunt Eunice crossed her arms.

Uncle Roy heaved himself from his chair and, like a little boy who'd been banished to his room, took his time leaving. Fifteen minutes later, he returned with a grin on his face. "I might have to join Summer in her crime solving. That was easy. Fred said Mae Belle had an inheritance left to her by her grandmother.

"She wouldn't share the amount or bank information with her mother, and now Claudia is determined to get her hands on it. Seems they're a bit short of cash, and Claudia doesn't want to wait until a lawyer tells her whether or not Mae Belle was still angry enough to leave everything to someone else."

"You did good." Aunt Eunice planted a kiss on his cheek.

"If there's money, there's paperwork. We ought to clear things up tomorrow."

"Except for finding her killer. I doubt we'll find them in Mae Belle's apartment." I rose from the sofa and shuddered, taking Ethan's hand in mine. "I'm walking Ethan out."

He gave me a startled look and allowed me to pull him to his feet.

We stepped onto the front porch, and I leaned against the banister. "Sorry if I seemed abrupt. I just needed to get out of there. It all seems a bit. . .cold, doesn't it? I mean we just buried Mae Belle, and her mother is ready to empty her apartment."

Ethan wrapped his arms around my waist, warding off the cool air. "Money is a powerful motivator. You know that from the last two mysteries you got involved in. Greed makes people do terrible things."

"If Mae Belle had money, she's hidden away any sign of it very thoroughly."

Ethan tilted my face to his and kissed me. "Good night, Tink. I'll see you tomorrow night."

I went to bed that night with a troubled spirit. While we searched for information on a phantom bank account, a murderer walked free.

Dressed in jeans and a sweatshirt, I joined my aunts in the kitchen at the awful hour of 6:00 a.m. On a Saturday, no less. Very little coffee remained in the pot, one slice of toast sat cold in the toaster, and we were out of milk for cereal.

I glared at Aunt Claudia who sat with a large bowl and three slices of butter-oozing toast. Who knew how much coffee the woman had consumed? The morning did not promise a good day.

I drank the last of the bitter coffee, wolfed down the piece of dry toast, grabbed my purse, then marched toward the front door. "Let's go.

Daylight's wasting."

My mood had not improved by the time I followed the others to the duplex Mae Belle rented. Sometime earlier, Aunt Eunice had found time to collect boxes, bags, and make signs with the words Keep, Donate, Sell, and Throw Away.

Had the woman gone to bed at all last night? The neighbor, who also happened to be the manager, let us into the apartment. I gasped. Our job would take forever. Mae Belle's home was as crowded and gaudy as her wedding shop. By her wardrobe and out-of-date hairstyle, along with the fifteen-year-old car she'd driven, I assumed she had no money. By the looks of the first room, she had cash once upon a time, and had spent every penny.

"Goodness!" Aunt Eunice clutched a hand to her bosom.

"Where do we start?"

I grabbed a box. "We each take a room. I'll start with the bedroom and bath, you take the kitchen, and Aunt Claudia can have this room."

I loved taking charge. Very few events in my life left me feeling like I knew what I was doing. Cleaning out closets and purging drawers was a pleasure. Most of the time, I got a little carried away and, to Aunt Eunice's dismay, threw out more than I should. I looked forward to tossing the majority of Mae Belle's garish belongings.

Clothes went straight into the donation box. Bedding and decorations into the boxes for a garage sale. Aunt Claudia ought to be happy about that. Whatever cash we made would go to her, being Mae Belle's closest living relative other than quiet

Uncle Fred. There was very little to throw away.

With my first boxes full, I hefted one and headed to the living room. "Hey!" I dropped the box I carried and ducked as a book sailed toward me.

"What are you doing?" It looked as if a hurricane had blown through. Aunt Claudia had done everything *except* sort and pack. I'd had enough.

"Stop. We know you're looking for something you think Mae Belle possessed. Don't you think it would be easier to find something if you went through her belongings with care and precision? She was your daughter, after all." So much for maternal instincts. "Show some respect."

"Don't talk to me in that tone of voice, young lady." She held up a hand. "Help me up."

I rolled my eyes. "I don't mean to be disrespectful, but. . ." *Yes, I did. Forgive me, Lord.* "You're making more work for us instead of helping." I planted my feet and tugged. The nerve of the woman.

"You just want it for yourself." She glared at me.

"Want what?" The beginning of a headache knocked between my eyes.

Aunt Claudia fell onto the sofa. The springs protested beneath the sudden onslaught of her weight. "When my mama died last year, she left Mae Belle ten thousand dollars. I need that money. Fred and I are barely scraping by. It should have been mine anyway. She was my mama, and Mae Belle had been nothing but an ungrateful little twit."

It took all y willpower, and a sharp bite to my tongue, to hold back the ranting I wanted to release on the woman. I dug my fingernails into the palms of my hands.

"Then Aunt Eunice and I will help you look. But from all the things crowded in here, I doubt there's any money left." I shoved an empty box into her hands. "Sort through this room, and maybe we'll get lucky."

Good grief. I retrieved my dropped carton and stacked it in a corner. Why couldn't I be at Summer Confections drowning in chocolate?

With a deep sigh, I moved back to the bedroom and resumed my search. In a shoe box on the top shelf of the closet, I discovered Mae Belle's bank statements and an envelope of photos. I was right. Mae Belle had spent all but a few hundred dollars. I'd let Aunt Eunice be the one to spill that particular bit of news to her sister.

I flipped through the photos. In every snapshot, Mae Belle posed with Lewis Anderson, the funeral director. And from the way they had their arms wrapped around each other, they were not strangers. *Oh what tangled webs we weave.*

10

Leaning back on my haunches, I studied the photos further. Why would Lewis lie about knowing Mae Belle?

I'd have to do a little more searching into the man. With Mae Belle dead, the man's lies could hide a sinister motive for denying that he knew her. Maybe Aunt Eunice could tell me something about him. She knew almost everything about everyone in Mountain Shadows.

I stuffed the photos in my pocket and the papers back in the shoe box. Why wait for Aunt Eunice to spill the beans when my tongue ran like a raging fire? "Aunt Claudia?" I marched into the living room. "Here's Mae Belle's bank statements.

There's only a few hundred dollars left. Apparently she used the money to start her business and furnish this apartment. Once her belongings are sold, you should get a couple hundred more."

For the first time since she stepped off the plane, my aunt showed signs of grief in the lines of her face and the slump of

her shoulders. She brushed off the skirt of her muumuu and struggled to her feet. "Oh. Well, that's it then. Guess Fred and I will be heading home tomorrow. Y'all can send what comes of all this to us in the mail." She waddled down the hall and into the bathroom, closing the door behind her.

Aunt Eunice poked her head around the corner. "Well, I never. I'm embarrassed to say Claudia's my sister. And now she expects us to finish this mess." She withdrew.

I shrugged and shook my head. If I'd learned anything in the past few months, it was that people continue to astound you. They often did the weirdest things at the oddest times. I'd never get use to the selfishness of humankind. That would always stump me.

The photos crackled in my pocket. I joined my aunt in the kitchen. "What do you know about Lewis Anderson?"

"Huh?" She paused while removing dishes from the cupboard.

"I'm curious. I'd never met him before the funeral arrangements. Is he new to town?"

"Fairly new." She wrapped a plate in a sheet of newspaper and placed it in a box. "Married with a couple of kids. Moved here from farther south. Close to the Texas border, I think. Why?"

Married? That would explain the secrecy. "Is he newly married? Are the children his?"

"Been with the same woman for about ten years is what I heard." Aunt Eunice slammed the cupboard door and opened another one. "Why all the questions?"

"You know me, as nosy as they come."

"Yes, I do. That's what worries me. What are

you up to now?" She pierced me with her slate blue gaze.

"Just a hunch I need to follow up on. I'll fill you in later. Mind if I take off for a bit?"

Aunt Eunice planted her pudgy fists on plump hips. "Don't go getting into any trouble. Uncle Roy and Ethan are working. They can't save you right now, and Joe has a crime to solve."

So did I. "Nothing serious, Aunt Eunice. I promise. I just need to check on someone."

I snatched my purse from where I'd dropped it on the kitchen table, slung my tote bag over my shoulder, and sprinted out the door before she could stop me.

Mae Belle had only lived in Mountain Shadows less than a year. If Lewis had been married for ten years, then why was he hanging all over my cousin in pictures that clearly were recent?

I slid behind the wheel of my Sonata. The web surrounding Mae Belle's murder seemed to become more tangled with each discovery. When Ethan and I had stumbled on the diamonds buried beneath my rosebush, and when I'd discovered the body of that carnival worker hanging in her shower, I'd solved those cases by luck, searching out clues, and lots of prayer. I'd stumbled into danger and been rescued by Ethan and Joe.

The next mystery, I'd managed to outwit the man trying to kill me. But it had been a group of high school football players who had saved Ethan. This time would be different. I'd use my brain and skill the entire time and wouldn't fall into the traps of the past.

Sure, I'd been smart, witty, and quick thinking when danger reared its ugly head, but this time, I'd solve this murder by pure intelligence. *Before* circumstances got dire.

I turned the ignition and burned rubber from the driveway of Mae Belle's apartment. The thought that I'd promised to share any information I dug up with Joe threatened to dispel some of my enthusiasm.

Regardless, I'd made a promise to Mae Belle. One I intended to keep. I'd give Joe the photos later.

I glanced down at my dust-covered clothes. Not appropriate attire for interviewing someone who appeared as distinguished as Lewis, but adulterers didn't deserve any better. Not in my book. Well, I knew what the Bible said about judging your fellow man. I said a prayer of repentance and squared my shoulders.

A t the funeral home, I sat in the parking lot and stared at the heavy oak doors. I needed to remain impartial. Lewis was a suspect. Nothing more. I should view him as such and not let my mouth get the best of me. *Help me, Lord. Don't let my tongue be a torrent of destruction.* With a deep breath, I cut the engine and shoved open my door.

Inside, the same made-up, heavily perfumed woman greeted me as at Mae Belle's funeral. After I'd asked to speak with Lewis, she informed me that "Mr. Anderson" was in the back garden. I held back a shiver.

The crypts I passed on my way outside gave me the heebie jeebies. The eyes of a stone angel seemed to follow my every move, and I gave a marble gargoyle a wide berth. Lewis sat on a wrought iron bench, hands folded, head down. Praying for forgiveness, perhaps?

"Mr. Anderson, may I speak with you?"

"Miss Meadows." He sighed and raised his head. "I'd be honored."

I withdrew the photos and handed them to him. "I found these in Mae Belle's apartment."

His breath released in a groan. "Ah, yes."

"Would you care to explain?" I perched on the corner of the bench. "You denied knowing her earlier."

"It went beyond knowing. I loved her."

"You're married to someone else."

"In name only, Miss Meadows." He handed back all the photos but one. The picture in his hand showed the two of them laughing, cocktail glasses in hand. Mason said Mae Belle took offense to alcohol. I really should've gotten to know my cousin better growing up. Oklahoma wasn't that far away.

"We took this one on our six-month anniversary. Such a fun-loving woman."

Mae Belle? Were we talking about the same woman? "Do you mind me asking how the two of you met?"

Lewis closed his eyes. "She browsed the aisles at Grandma's Story Corner. Our eyes met over a table of reference books. It was love at first sight."

"You are still married, Mr. Anderson. And I'd like that photo back, please. The authorities will be very interested in these."

"Surely you don't think I killed her, do you?" He clenched his fists, the knuckles white against the dark of his pants.

I shrugged. "Maybe to hide your affair? Wouldn't be the first time someone reacted that way."

He bolted to his feet, startling me. I tumbled backward off the bench, landing in a patch of ivy. Thank the Lord it wasn't poison ivy. To the man's credit, he held out a hand to help me. Or capture me. I wasn't taking the chance. I declined his offer and rose to resume my seat.

"I would never hurt that sweet woman." He sat. His shoulders drooped. "We had future plans. Plans to marry, once my children were grown, but Mae Belle grew impatient. We argued the day before she. . .passed. That's the last time I saw her."

"Did she threaten to tell your wife about the two of you? Is that why you argued?"

"May I please have the photos?" He held out his hand.

I shook my head and leaned forward to shove them into the back pocket of my jeans. "I'm afraid I can't give them to you."

He lunged at me, forcing me to slide off the bench again. "Those pictures cannot get around. It'll ruin me. And think of the pain to my family."

My legs wouldn't cooperate. My feet slipped on the cobblestone walkway. I crawled away from him, putting a fountain between the two of us. So much for staying out of danger.

Using a statue for balance, I got to my feet. "You should have thought of that earlier. One more step, Mr. Anderson, and I will scream."

He took the step, my scream came out as more of a croak, and I jumped back. His countenance fell. Tears ran down his cheeks, and he buried his face in his hands. For a moment I felt compassion, then shook it off. I'd reserve judgment until he was either proved innocent or guilty. I darted from the garden and back to my car.

I broke a speed record racing to the police station and screeched to a halt in front of the building. An officer frowned as I exited the car. I gave a sheepish grin and marched inside.

"Hello, Ruby." I greeted one of Aunt Eunice's oldest and dearest friends, Ruby Colville.

"Good afternoon, Summer. Accused any innocent people lately?" That woman never had forgiven me for thinking she was behind the diamond heist. A perfectly normal assumption given the fact she'd come into some expensive things at the time. Perfectly honest mistake. Diamonds showed up beneath my rosebush and around her neck. What else would I think?

Then I'd gone against her wishes when she wanted to kick the carnival out of town in September because they'd been short of cash. Not their fault. They'd been robbed and lost a couple of employees to a madman on a killing spree.

"Is Joe in?"

Ruby motioned her head toward his office.

"Thanks." I shoved aside the waist-high swinging door and made my way past the curious glances of the few officers Mountain Shadows employed.

Joe sat behind his desk, working through a pile of paperwork. After noticing me standing in the doorway, he turned the papers facedown.

Without waiting for an invitation, I sat in the chair opposite his green metal desk. I fished the photos from my pocket and tossed them in front of him.

"What are these?" Joe flipped through them. "Why are they wrinkled?"

"They're leads. I had them in my pocket. While making the funeral arrangements, I asked Lewis Anderson if he knew Mae Belle. He said no. The pictures say otherwise."

"Why would you ask him that?"

"Because he had tears in his eyes."

"Tears in his eyes."

"Stop repeating everything I say." I folded my arms.

"I don't."

"Yes, you do. All the time." I moved to take back the snapshots. Joe held them out of my reach. "I questioned Lewis a few minutes ago. He and Mae Belle were having an affair. He all but attacked me to keep me from bringing the pictures to you."

"An affair? Mae Belle didn't seem the type. You just can't tell with people, can you?"

"Guess not." I crossed my legs, feeling pleased with myself. "What do you think about my investigative skills now?"

Joe leaned his arms on the desk. "Not bad. For an amateur. That puts Lewis as our number-one unsub, if your information is correct."

"The pictures don't lie."

"Pictures lie all the time, but these do look suspicious. Doesn't mean he killed her though."

"I also suspect Mason White. He threatened me."

"How so?"

"By telling me to be careful because Mae Belle got it in the back." I was doing great. Keeping my cool. Firing clues like that soldier person who manned a machine gun.

"Doesn't mean a thing." Joe slid the photos beneath the stack on his desk. "You're overstepping your boundaries again, Summer. Meddling won't keep you safe."

I frowned. "Yes, it does. It makes him another suspect. Didn't you see his name in the appointment book?"

"Along with a few others." Joe's eyes flashed. "I'm doing my job, Summer. But I do appreciate the photos. They put another spin on things. Remember. . .You're the candy maker. I'm the cop. Don't overstep your boundaries."

"Or what? You'll arrest me again?"

"If I have to."

"You are so unappreciative. After all I've—"

"Am I interrupting something?"

I turned and saw the person who belonged to another name in Mae Belle's book.

Renee Richards, Mountain Shadows's homecoming queen.

84

11

What could Miss Glamour Queen want with Joe? I eyed her gemstone-decorated jeans and low-cut silk blouse, instantly regretting that I hadn't taken the time to clean up before making the trip downtown. Even in a place as small as Mountain Shadows, our paths didn't often cross.

When they did, I wondered why Renee stuck around. A larger city would offer more in the way of entertainment. I tried melting into the seat.

"Summer." Jade eyes pierced me with the strength of a warrior's sword. Every bit as cold and biting.

"Renee."

"I hope I'm not interrupting anything." The smirk on her face said otherwise. "Ruby said, since it was Summer, I could come on in."

Joe leaned back in his chair. "No problem. We were just finished."

The bum. I'd tattle to April if he didn't put his eyes back in his head. "Actually, we weren't finished." I tried making Renee squirm with my own gaze, but all I got in return was the arching of her finely tweezed eyebrows. "I recently saw your name in Mae Belle's appointment book. Crossed out. You were obviously a client of hers. Why weren't you at the funeral?"

"Summer." Joe leaned forward. "We *are* finished. Sorry about that, Miss Richards."

She waved a manicured hand. "No problem, officer. I'd hired Mae Belle to plan my, uh, birthday party and. . ."

"Your *thirtieth* birthday." I smiled in satisfaction as her face flushed.

Her lips tightened. "Mae Belle made a total sham of the whole thing. So, understandably, I canceled the next appointment with her. I had planned on hiring her for my fiancé's homecoming until the complete mess she made of my birthday."

"A sham? How? Did she put up a banner stating your age?" I giggled at my wittiness then clamped my mouth shut at the look on Renee's face. I might've crossed the line.

Renee's eyes narrowed like a feline's, flashing green. A shiver ran up my spine as she stepped closer and towered over me. I slumped in the chair.

"Mae Belle made a mess of everything she attempted. Someone apparently got tired of her ineptitude."

What happened to Southern charm? We ladies from the South were supposed to be oozing with it. Or at least cover our animosity with sugary words and a "Bless your heart."

I bolted to my feet, sending the chair crashing backward into the wall. "Did you hear that, Joe? A motive for murder. Add Renee to the list of suspects."

"Oh please. You're still as dramatic as you were in high school." Renee folded her arms.

Joe's gaze flickered across her emphasized chest then back to me. Good for him. "Summer, please leave. Miss Richards has business with me, and she can't accomplish it with you here."

"Fine." I tried to grab the pictures from his desk. I'd get to the bottom of her visit later.

"Oh no you don't. These are now evidence." He slammed his hand down, pinning the photos to his desk.

Perfect. I should have made copies before bringing them over. I whirled, caught my foot on the rung of the chair, and went to my knees. The impact sent a tremor of pain through my body.

Renee snickered. "Still graceful, I see."

Joe jumped to his feet and darted around his desk.

Face red, I got to my feet, shrugging off Joe's chivalrous offer of help. I waited to rub the aching joint until I hobbled outside where I leaned against the warm brick of the building. Just once, I'd like to make an exit with a statement other than "big klutz exiting."

I needed chocolate to make me feel better, or Ethan's arms around me. Maybe his lips on mine. Or a big fat clue that moved me closer to my goal of finding Mae Belle's killer.

I opted to wait for Renee. To kill time, I pulled my notebook from the tote bag and slid down the wall to rest on the sidewalk. I fished for a pen, opened the notebook, and, with a flourish, wrote Renee's name on my suspect list.

Right under Lewis Anderson. Sherry Grover because of her lack of remorse when Mae Belle died, Lewis Anderson for lying to me, Renee Richards for her subtle threats, and Mason White because. . .I wasn't sure about him, but there had to be a reason.

My list grew, and I'd definitely be keeping an eye on all of them. I'd have to get April to help me, or Aunt Eunice. Between the three of us, we'd have this case solved in no time.

A shadow fell across me. I glanced up to see Renee smirking down at me. "What are you doing on the ground?"

I pushed to my feet. "Waiting for you. You finished quick."

"What are you writing?"

"Personal stuff." I shoved the notebook and pen back in my bag. "Where were you on the day Mae Belle died?"

"Stop digging, Summer." Renee turned and sashayed away, the heels of her boots beating against the sidewalk.

In comparison, my gym shoes were as silent as a wraith. "What did you need to see Joe about?"

She spun. I stopped so fast that I found myself closer to her than I'd ever been before.

"You are as tenacious as a bulldog." I didn't think Renee meant the statement as a compliment. "That is none of your business, Summer. As for where I was when Mae Belle was killed—also none of your business, but you won't stop until I answer, will you? I was on a satellite call with Bill."

"Any alibis?" Who told her when, exactly, Mae

Belle had been attacked? Excitement raced through me. Another fact for my notes.

She sneered. "Still fancy yourself a detective? Why couldn't you have permanently gotten lost in the fair's fun house? Would have saved everyone a lot of grief."

Why did she have to bring that up? Getting lost in the fun house at the annual county fair had not been my idea of fun. I hated clowns, not to mention getting chased by a madman with a gun through the maze of mirrors. Renee was plain mean to mention the incident. "So you think I deserve a letter opener in the back?"

"Look, Summer. I'm not saying any such thing, but I'm not going to stand aside and let you dirty my name around town just because I didn't like the poor service Mae Belle gave me. Take your snoopy little nose somewhere else."

Okay. Those words stopped me. Sounded like another threat. First Mason, now Renee. Not being a stranger to danger, I didn't fall into a terrified faint, but the words did give me pause. I'd have to be sneakier about obtaining my information.

I turned and headed back to the candy store. I'd been so surprised to see Renee that I'd forgotten to ask Joe whether he had any leads on my threatening letter.

I entertained the thought of stopping by the station again, then shrugged it off. I'd ask him later. He'd be over for dinner, along with April. And Ethan. That bright thought put a skip in my step. A skip with a limp. My knee throbbed all the way to my car.

Several customers browsed the store when I entered, and I breathed a sigh of relief that Aunt Eunice wasn't spending the entire day at Mae Belle's apartment. If I could make it to the dipping machine before Aunt Eunice saw me limping, I might be free of her questioning.

The marble slab we used for candy making hid beneath a mound of what looked like new fan mail. I sighed and wondered when I'd have time to go through it. I grabbed an ice pack from the freezer. I'd study my notes while I waited for the chocolate to melt.

With the bag of ice balanced precariously on my knee beneath the worktable, I spread papers in front of me. Two names from the appointment book had been questioned, leading me nowhere except into more threats. That left Hubert Smith, Edna Mobley, and Larry Bell. All middle-aged or older. They couldn't be too difficult, could they? And I didn't want to forget Sherry. She needed more investigating if for nothing else but her lack of compassion.

Remorse riddled me. I'd grown bitter and presumptuous since Mae Belle's death. Being unfriendly did not make a murderer. To have chosen to work for Mae Belle, Sherry must have desperately needed a job. She could have a difficult life or suffer from self-esteem issues. Who was I to judge?

"You going to dip with that melted chocolate or daydream all day?" Aunt Eunice plunked down a tray of chocolate creams.

"Just going over my notes."

"Getting anywhere?"

"No." I stood. The ice pack fell to the floor with a *thunk.*

Aunt Eunice peered beneath the table. "What are you using the ice pack for?" She straightened. "Did you hurt yourself? Where have you been?"

Remembering my new vow of honesty, I said, "First I went to question Larry Anderson about photos I found in Mae Belle's apartment. During our discussion, he admitted to having an affair with my dear cousin. Then I took the pictures to Joe as evidence of Larry's lying. I ran into Renee Richards, who said Mae Belle deserved what she got, and I fell leaving Joe's office."

My aunt's eyelashes fluttered like a moth around a flame. "You've been busy."

"And got nowhere. Everyone's a suspect, it seems." I limped over and sat on the stool behind the dipping machine. If making delectable chocolates didn't calm me, nothing would. "Did you finish with the apartment?"

"Almost. Claudia got tired." Aunt Eunice plopped onto another stool. "Lord forgive me, but I'll be glad when she leaves tomorrow. I do feel sad for her, though. I can't imagine a child of mine dying with hateful words spoken and no salvaging the relationship."

"Especially when the loved one was a murder victim." I swirled a *C* on the just-dipped candy.

Time raced by. It'd already been a week. I'd step up my investigating and visit Larry Bell's farm tonight. There had to be a reason that a single, reclusive farmer with no marriage prospects

would've needed Mae Belle's services.
I'd go with or without company.

92

12

Aunt Eunice loaded the kitchen table with fried chicken, mashed sweet potatoes, and corn bread with cracklins. Complete with homemade muscadine jelly. While my tongue salivated, my backside grew larger just looking at the food.

Aunt Claudia moped at one end of the table, her mouth forming a perfect upside down horseshoe, while the two uncles argued politics, Joe and April whispered like two love-struck teenagers, and Ethan's smoldering eyes followed my every move as I helped Aunt Eunice. She must have been in a spat with her sister earlier, because they weren't speaking to each other.

Ethan's glances warmed me, caused my face to heat and my thoughts to veer in directions that weren't proper. Thank

goodness people surrounded us. Maybe we should elope. Tonight.

I whispered for him to stop and set a plate in front of him. He gave me a smile that started at one corner and took its time getting to the other. A dimple winked. My heart stuttered. I didn't think it was possible for my face to burn any hotter. I prayed a look from him would always affect me this way.

Ethan stood and pulled out the chair beside him for me to sit. "Your face is red." His words tickled the hair at the nape of my neck.

"Stop it." I reached for the glass of iced tea beside my plate.

"Stop what?" He placed his lips next to my ear. His breath tickled.

"You know what. Behave." I swatted him away. "What are you doing after dinner?"

"I'm going to kiss you until you can't stand up, then I've got to head home to grade papers. You?"

"Hang out with April. Girl stuff." I had yet to ask April.

Seeing as how she giggled with Joe, I'd probably have to twist her arm to get her away from him.

"Uh-huh." Ethan moved back to his seat and lifted a chicken leg. He took a bite, his gaze focused on mine.

"Really. We'll most likely head into town." There I went with the half-truths again. How could this man love me? I turned to his sister across the table. "April, do you want to hang out later?"

She pulled her attention away from Joe. "Sure. Joe has to work." She turned back to her love.

I gave Ethan a smile.

He tilted his head. "That doesn't mean you aren't up to something."

"Nothing dangerous, I promise." I might as well come clean. "I'm going down the list of Mae

Belle's appointments. We aren't going to town, but away from it."

"Who's the target tonight?"

"Larry Bell."

Ethan's brow furrowed. "Okay, but you and April stay together. Don't do anything stupid."

I grinned. "You know me."

"Yes, I do."

***

"Where are we, and what are we doing here?" April leaned forward to peer out the front window of my car.

Larry Bell's farm, actually nothing more than a small ranch house and barn, seemed deserted beneath the full moon.

"We're investigating."

"Oh, Summer. I don't want to be wandering around in the dark, in a strange place, looking for a murderer. Besides, what happened to Claudia helping you find the killer of her 'baby'?" April's pale face shone from the light of the moon.

"She seems to have lost interest." I shrugged. "Besides, she's going home tomorrow. I'd rather be with you. Remember that time at church when you said you would be my sidekick?"

"That was before you almost got yourself killed. Twice. I don't think I'll do well with being kidnapped and shot at. Not to mention Joe will have a coronary."

We shoved open our doors and slid from the car. "Maybe you'll get lucky and no one will be home."

"I can only hope." April slammed her door. The

sound reverberated across the yard.

"Shh. We need the element of surprise."

April rolled her eyes. For a best friend, her behavior and her lack of a sense of adventure let me down. "Just follow my lead. You're only here for support. I'll do the talking." I gave her what I hoped was my most reassuring smile. She frowned and followed me onto the front porch.

After receiving no response from knocking, we peered through the front window into a room full of shadows. "Let's go around back."

April clutched my arm. A coyote howled in the distance. "How can you do this? I'm terrified. I should've got my cell phone out of your car. Oh no, I'm turning into you. You never remember your phone. At least then Joe would have been only the push of a button away."

"Stop being a baby. Do you know you're rambling?" I pulled free from her grasp and cupped my hands around my eyes to see through a grimy kitchen window. "You're in luck. I don't think anyone's home." I grasped the knob. The door pushed open with a turn of the knob.

"What are you doing? This is breaking and entering. Joe's going to be livid." April regained her death grip on my arm.

"You already said that, and we aren't breaking and entering. You're a real scaredy-cat, you know that? The door opened by itself. Mostly."

Something crunched under our feet as we stepped into the kitchen. I pulled my newest toy from the pocket of my jeans. A pink, pen-size flashlight. The beam revealed food crumbs on the floor, dirty dishes stacked in the sink, and grease splattered across the stove. This place definitely lacked a feminine touch.

I moved into the living room and stepped into a maze. Magazines and newspapers were stacked five feet high or more in every available inch of space, only leaving room to walk between them. Claustrophobia threatened before we took another step. I tried to pull my arm free of April.

"Let go of me, and take a look around."

"No way. I'm staying right beside you. This place gives me the creeps. I feel like a mouse in some weird science experiment. You know, like how long does it take to find the cheese? And *what* is that smell?" She gagged and pulled the neckline of her shirt over her nose.

"Most likely the several days' worth of dirty dishes piled in the kitchen. Spoiled food. And something else. . .like cat urine." I shone the light around the space we stood in, revealing nothing but towering paper walls.

"There's got to be something here to let me know what Larry's relationship with Mae Belle was." I led the way. A cat sailed over our heads, and I shrieked.

It landed on another stack of magazines and perched there like a phantom, yellow eyes glowing in the light.

"I'm going to throw up." April sniffled behind me. "I've never been more frightened in my entire life."

Horror. That was one of the things in life that terrified me the most: someone losing their dinner in front of me. Had Nancy Drew suffered like this with her friends? I didn't think so.

"I'll never let you talk me into another one of your adventures. Somebody hit me if I do. You're criminally insane, Summer."

I tuned her out. Obviously, April didn't know how to have fun.

Ta-da! At the end of one of the rows of magazines sat a battered desk and a computer. The little green light showed it was on. Now, if only Larry didn't use a password. . .

My fingers flew across the keyboard, and I held back a shout of triumph. He didn't. The man obviously didn't expect someone to snoop through his computer. Another few taps of the keys, and we were in. I scrolled down his history usage.

Chat room after chat room. I clicked on one and read as quickly as my eyes could scan the words. Who was Lola? Whoever she was, she laid on the flowery talk. Obviously Larry had an Internet sweetie.

"We shouldn't be doing this." April leaned over my shoulder. "Eew. Such talk. Who is this guy?"

"A little mouse of a man. I only saw him once. At Mac Bello's funeral."

The sound of the front door squeaking open reached us. The car! I'd left it out front. Nothing like announcing our presence. I shoved April. "Run! Out the back door."

She spun and bumped into a tower of magazines. I reached for the wobbling mass of paper then dodged to safety as it fell, knocking my flashlight from my hand. On my knees I dug through the papers and tried to stifle my giggles. A sense of déjà vu overcame me. I'd done the same crawl and search in the fun house at the fair.

"Snowball?" Larry's voice sounded shrill in the dark room. "Are you knocking things over again?"

April tugged at me. "Come on. Please." Her harsh whisper seemed loud as it bounced off the towers around us.

"Wait." Found it. I jumped to my feet and clicked off the light. Which way? I grabbed April's hand and pulled her to the right. Dead end. We swerved in another direction and found ourselves in the bedroom. Piles of laundry blocked our path. We bolted for the window.

"Bad kitty." Larry's voice followed us. "Making more work for Daddy."

With a heave, I shoved the window open and slammed my palm against the screen. It fell to the ground with a clatter.

April barreled into me, sending us both over the sill and crashing into the bushes outside. I landed on my sore knee and bit my lip to prevent myself from groaning. I struggled to my feet, pulled the window closed, and did an awkward limp-sprint kind of lurch around the corner of the house.

April stayed close behind. My knee throbbed again, worse than when I'd fallen in Joe's office. I held up a hand for April to stop.

We doubled over, breathing labored. My heart beat a thousand times its normal rate. I couldn't stop the grin that split my face. What a rush. This sneaking into places could easily become habit forming.

"What. . .is so. . .funny?" April stood, chest heaving, hands on her hips.

"Don't tell me you didn't enjoy that. Wouldn't I make a great cat burglar?"

"Almost getting caught snooping through someone's personal things? That's not my idea of fun, and cat burglars are silent. Come and go without being seen or heard."

"Don't be such a stick-in-the-mud. Come on."

"Where are we going? Home? And why are you limping again? We could have been killed. Lord, help us. My brother is going to annihilate me."

"I told Ethan where we were going, and I banged my knee again falling out the window. I'll be fine. Stop exaggerating." I glanced over my shoulder. "Larry's seen the car, April. We have to say *something* to him."

"What?"

"I'll be honest."

"That'll be a first."

Another comedian. "I'll tell him about finding his name in the appointment book, it seems to have worked with everyone else, and that we were wandering around looking for him."

"Well, there's your chance."

A light cut a swath through the darkness. Grabbing April's hand, I yanked her onto the porch. With any luck, he'd think we'd been there the entire time. I plopped into a battered wicker love seat, pulled April down beside me, and scanned the man for any sign of a weapon. A habit I'd developed since the last two cases I'd worked on. He seemed to hold nothing but a massive flashlight. *Please,*

Lord, don't let him bash my head in.

"May I help you?" He shone the light in my eyes.

I held up a hand to shield my face and stepped forward. "Mr. Bell, I'm Summer Meadows, cousin of Mae Belle. I saw you at the funeral and wanted to pass on the family's thanks for your attending. I'm sure it would have meant a lot to my cousin."

"Couldn't stand the woman. I had business with the dentist. Needed to set up an appointment. That girlfriend of his don't always answer the phone after hours. Not everyone works nine to five, you know."

"O–kay." *Strange place to make an appointment.* I shrugged off April's clutching hands. What was with the clinginess?

"I thought you were going to be honest," she whispered.

"I am." My answer came out as a hiss. I turned back to Mr. Bell. "May I ask what was the problem you had with my cousin?"

"Nosy, meddling, lying woman." He spat in the dirt at his feet. "Got what she had coming to her, if you ask me."

13

Burrowed beneath the down-filled comforter on my bed, I wanted nothing to do with any more investigating. Or wondering what the list of suspects thought about my late cousin.

Could Mae Belle, or any one woman, possibly have been so despised? What if people felt that way about me? I'd been warned plenty of times what happens to people who put their nose where it doesn't belong.

I flopped onto my side and glared at the clock. Five a.m. The only reassuring thought about the day was Aunt Claudia's leaving.

In a fit of super-sleuthing, I'd made an appointment with another person on my list. The dentist, Hubert Smith.

A fate worse than death, as far as I was concerned. With a groan I tossed aside my warm blankets. Might as well get this day over with. It promised to be anything but a joy.

Aunt Eunice sat at the kitchen table, a silly grin on her face, as I padded into the room in my teddy bear slippers. Her giddy look made me nervous, and

I skirted a wide path on my way to the coffeepot.

Curiosity won. "Why are you so chipper this morning?"

"She's gone. Left first thing this morning." Aunt Eunice's eyes widened. "That sounded horrible, didn't it? Lord, forgive me, but I'm grateful my sister doesn't live close. Sad, too. I would've loved a sister who was also a friend."

I patted her on the shoulder as I passed. A mug of coffee warmed my hands. After sitting in a chair opposite my aunt, I inhaled the aroma. "Don't feel bad. It makes me sick that so many people disliked my cousin. She lived in Mountain Shadows almost a year.

"I should've gotten to know her better. Maybe I could've helped her. Everyone loves Joe, and I seem to be well liked, at least to my face and by people not on my suspect list, but poor Mae Belle." With a mother like hers, I guess she never had a chance.

"The Meadowses are one of the founding fathers of Mountain Shadows. Of course, we're well liked, but same as any other family, we'll have a black sheep or two. I'm sure your cousin left Oklahoma to get away from her mother."

My aunt pushed to her feet. "Enough of that. What are your plans for the day? There're more creams to be dipped. We're getting low on peanut brittle, and—"

"I've got a dentist appointment."

Aunt Eunice almost choked. "Are you all right? It isn't time for your cleaning."

"I made an appointment with Hubert Smith." I

blew into my mug.

"It seems like every time you get involved in a mystery, I end up doing more work at the store. I hope Ethan puts a stop to this nonsense once y'all are married."

A twinge of guilt tweaked my conscience. "Ethan will support me in whatever I choose to do."

"Humph." Aunt Eunice put her empty mug in the sink. "Keep on dreaming, sweetie. And I don't think Dr. Smith plays Disney theme songs in the background or gives you something to relax—just for a cleaning."

With those encouraging words, she left me alone.

***

Perspiration dotted my upper lip despite the crisp air. I wiped my damp hands on my pants. I should have stayed home and played a game of hide-and-seek with Truly. The lengths I'd go to keep a promise. *God, help me.*

With that prayer, I pulled open the brass-trimmed glass door, shivered in beat with the melodic jangle that played over my head, and shuffled toward the receptionist.

Things looked a little brighter when I read the name on her nameplate, Edna Mobley. Wasn't she the one who was once engaged to Hubert? Regardless, she was a name in Mae Belle's book.

I signed in. Edna gave me a tight-lipped smile in return and nodded toward the waiting area. Friendliness did not ooze from the woman or ease my trepidation about being here. I took a seat in a green-striped chair.

My hands shook harder. How would I question Hubert if I let him put dangerous tools in my mouth? And why was his *ex*-fiancée working for him?

Minutes ticked by, foretelling my doom. I couldn't do this. No way. Bolting to my feet, I headed for the door.

"Miss Meadows? Dr. Smith is ready for you."

Her words had the same effect as a bucket of ice water on my head. Taking a deep breath, I willed my limbs to stop their trembling, turned, and forced a smile on my face. Maybe if I kept him talking, we'd never get to the actual exam.

A pert girl who didn't look old enough to be out of high school shepherded me into a chair, laid a million-pound x-ray jacket over me, shoved what felt like stiff cardboard in my mouth, cutting into my gums, then told me to hold still.

I rolled my eyes. Like, I'd actually planned on dancing a jig.

That only happened once. Under the influence of the wonderful laughing gas. I'd giggled and hallucinated myself dancing a lively Irish dance with Ethan on the overhead light. I willed myself back to that place.

Torture accomplished, she removed her death preparation tools and informed me Dr. Smith would be right in. Not if I could escape first. I leaped from the chair, clutched my purse, and ran into the man, hard enough to clunk our heads together. Stars swam before my eyes.

With one hand on his forehead and the other gripping my arm, Dr. Smith led me back to the chair. "Are you all right? That was quite a wallop we got."

He called the assistant back in and before my eyes could focus, there were metal utensils in my mouth. Cotton balls and floss rested on my chest.

Horror. There was no getting away now. I clutched the armrests tight enough to lock my finger joints and grunted in response to endless mundane questions. How did they expect me to answer with my mouth full?

"You've got remarkably clean teeth, Miss Meadows. When was the last time you had them cleaned?"

One month. I held up a finger. How much was this day's sleuthing going to cost me?

"A year? Remarkable. You really take care of these little babies. They look as if you just had them done. You might want to lay off the coffee. I see a few stains here."

Stains? Oh my. Vanity is slain. I stared into the man's oversize hazel eyes. His bottle-glass spectacles reminded me of a bookworm I'd seen in a cartoon once.

He squeezed my shoulder. "I'll leave you in the capable hands of my assistant. She doesn't hurt too much."

Great. I'd endured unbelievable torture and hadn't gathered one clue. With my eyes squeezed shut, I drifted to my happy place until the dental hygienist finished. When she removed the bib and told me I was done, I almost cried tears of relief.

Back in the reception area, I paused. Hubert leaned against the counter, speaking in a soft tone to

Edna. Bright circles of scarlet dotted the woman's thin cheeks. Maybe the love wasn't dead after all. Before I got caught lurking behind a potted silk plant, I pasted another smile on my face and

stepped forward.

"Y'all make a cute couple." I tried not comparing them with Mr. Toad and a sparrow, but their physical characteristics made it impossible. "I heard through the grapevine you'd been engaged once."

Edna's lips pursed. I immediately wished for a stronger hinge on my tongue.

"Once is correct." Edna straightened an already neat stack of papers in front of her.

"A situation that could be remedied." Hubert placed a hand over the woman's fidgety ones.

"We'd have to begin the planning all over again." Edna raised a brown-eyed gaze to Hubert. "I'm not sure I can go through that."

"You used Mae Belle, right?"

They both turned to glare at me. Did my cousin have *any* satisfied customers? "I'm sorry. It's really none of my business, but I find myself now having to plan my own wedding. A challenge, but fun."

"If your cousin had done her job properly, we'd be married now." Edna stood with enough force to shove her rolling office chair against a file cabinet. "I'm not getting any younger."

"All the more reason to take Hubert up on his offer."

I withdrew my insurance card. The company probably wouldn't pay, since I'd had the same services performed last month, but it would prolong my time in here. "You could always elope."

"Miss Meadows, my Edna had her heart set on the wedding of her dreams. Neither of us has ever been married. Mae Belle flubbed the plans, taking way too long to get colors, payment, that sort of thing to the companies we'd chosen." Hubert folded his arms. "No one could meet the deadline."

"If she managed to do any planning at all, it's less work for you to do. I'm sure I could get any notes she might have made."

I gnawed my lower lip. The tension in the air threatened to suffocate me. Hubert seemed nice, but I detected the layer of steel beneath his pudginess. Edna's demeanor chilled the air.

She handed me my card. "I'll never forgive that woman. I've looked forward to my wedding my entire life."

"She's dead." I slipped my insurance information back in my purse. "Forgiveness would be for you—not Mae Belle. My suggestion to you both—if marriage is your dream, then get married." With a flick of my hair, I marched out of the office, thankful I'd managed to make it half a day without getting a threat against my safety.

Around the corner, leaning against the car beside mine, Renee Richards and Mason White stood close in conversation. For someone engaged to another man, Renee looked cozy.

She giggled at something Mason whispered in her ear. He moved closer. If I searched hard enough, I might be able to find light between the two of them.

They jerked apart when I hit the panic button on

my car fob. "Sorry. Wrong button."

Mason grinned and folded his arms. "If it isn't Little Miss Sleuth."

"Yeah, Summer, how's the detective work?" The two roared with laughter.

"Going great. The two of you are at the top of my suspect list." And with those unwise words, I opened my door and slid behind the wheel. Renee and Mason gaped like a couple of beached bass.

14

The Lord needed to bang me in the head. Knock some sense into my hard noggin. Why did I tell them they were suspects? Did I have a death wish buried so deep into my psyche that I couldn't find it?

I turned the key in the ignition, left the couple standing in the alley where I'd foolishly chosen to park my vehicle, and headed to the store. Aunt Eunice would be waiting to grill me for details. Wasn't enduring pain at the hands of a maniacal dental assistant enough punishment for one day?

A glance in my rearview mirror caused me to press harder on the gas. Mason White followed in a silver Mercedes. His white grin shone like a jack-o'-lantern's.

Lord, please don't let me wreck another Sonata. Not that I wasn't tired of driving the same style of car for the last three years. But the last time my car came face-to-face with a tree, I'd spent the night at the hospital. Still had the scar to show for it. Thank goodness for swoop bangs.

Maybe it was just a coincidence Mason

followed so closely. So what if he lived in the other direction. I sped up.

He copied. I stomped the brakes and whipped the wheel to take the car to the side of the road. Gravel flew as I stomped on the brakes. Mason did the same.

I rolled up my window and locked the door, keeping my gaze on my rearview mirror. Mason sat and stared straight ahead. After what seemed like an eternity, he pulled back onto the highway, gave me a little wave, and headed in the direction we'd come.

Taking deep breaths, I willed my heartbeat to slow to normal. A tap on the window startled me. I yelped. Joe stood there, brow creased, hand still poised to tap his high school class ring on the glass. I pushed the button to lower the glass separating us.

"Car trouble?" Joe removed his hat. "Pop the hood. I'll take a look."

"Mason White followed me from town. Scared me to death."

"What makes you think he was following you?"

"He doesn't live in this direction, and I just had an altercation with him and Renee Richards."

Joe sighed. "That doesn't mean anything, Summer. You're overreacting, as usual. What kind of an altercation? They aren't going to come to me to put a restraining order on you, are they?"

"Forget it. When I wind up dead, you'll be sorry. Watch your feet." I stomped the gas pedal and spun gravel. He jumped back as I sped onto the highway. *Restraining order indeed.*

When I entered the candy store, Aunt Eunice

stood frowning over a tray of just-dipped creams. "Why don't mine look as nice as yours?"

The dark chocolate looked milky with grayish white streaks in the swirls. "They've bloomed. Did you check the temperature of the chocolate before you dipped?"

"I turned the machine on, then we had a rush of customers. I can't do everything."

"The machine should have kept it tempered." I checked the thermostat. "Did you turn it up? The chocolate is too hot."

She planted her fists on her hips. "I might have. I don't know how to use that thing. With you being gone all the time, we're getting backed up."

"I'll re-dip them. Let me put on my apron and clean out the machine. I'll stay late tonight."

"Then I have to stay, too."

"Why?"

"I promised Ethan and Joe. They don't want you alone. Not after you received that letter."

Hadn't anyone heard of locking doors? Even I could manage to turn a dead bolt. I slipped the apron over my head and headed to the sink to wash my hands. "No clues as to who sent it?"

"Nothing." She dumped the tray of creams in the trash. "Joe's frustrated. No clues to the letter and none regarding who murdered Mae Belle."

"Hey! I said I would re-dip those." Did she think chocolate grew on trees?

"Sorry." Aunt Eunice plopped on the stool. "How did your dentist appointment go?"

"Horrible." I plunged my hands into the ruined chocolate. If there had to be a mess to clean up, what could be better than this? The silky softness covering my hands soothed me, erasing the tension of my morning. "But things are getting better."

The chocolate dropped into the bowl beside the machine. "Why do you think Edna canceled the wedding after Mae Belle messed things up? It's plain to see she still cares for Hubert, and he's nuts about her."

"Edna is a strange bird. Wants things a certain way. If it doesn't happen, she's finished and doesn't want to put any more effort into it. Everyone around her has to pay for someone else's mistake." Aunt Eunice wiped around the dipper with a damp towel.

"She's been that way as long as I've known her. She ought to feel lucky that some man wants to spend his life with her. You should've seen her back in the day. She was a looker once upon a time. Had all the boys crazy about her."

My aunt giggled. "Although I managed to have my own following."

"Speaking of, I saw Renee and Mason in a very intimate pose in the alley where I parked my car." The chocolate plopped from my hands into the pan.

Aunt Eunice stopped her cleaning. "Why'd you park in the alley? Isn't there any sense in that head of yours? Do you remember what happened the last time? You were kidnapped and locked in a trunk."

"I didn't want to have to hunt for a parking space." And I'd parked in the alley lots of times since then. I think Aunt Eunice called me crazy beneath her breath.

She moved to light the flame on the gas stove. While I finished cleaning, she measured the ingredients for peanut brittle. We couldn't seem to keep the candy on the shelf. A blessing, really.

"Renee always has been a fickle little filly. With her man in Iraq, she's probably just playing around." Aunt Eunice poured corn syrup in the large copper vat.

I dropped chunks of fresh chocolate into the dipper. "I said something I probably shouldn't have."

"That would be a first." My aunt glanced at me. "What did you say?"

"I told them they were on my suspect list." At her incredulous look, I added, "She was being mean."

"You poor baby." She shook her head and muttered something about me being empty-headed.

I measured the raw Spanish peanuts into a bowl and set it on the table next to her. "She gets into my craw sometimes. I couldn't help myself. Besides, if you'd help me like you said you would, I might not get into as much trouble."

"Don't lay this on me, missy. I'm a busy woman."

Folding my arms, I leaned against the marble slab. "Mason White followed me halfway here, and Joe didn't do anything about it."

"Mason was just heading in the same direction."

"Then why did he turn and go the other way after I pulled over?"

"Probably just playing a game. He's a bit of a bully." She adjusted the flame on the stove. "That's what happens when your family's the richest in town."

The bell over the door rang, and a boy around the age of ten strolled in with a cardboard box under his arm. "Delivery."

I glanced at my aunt. She shrugged. We hadn't placed any orders, and the shoe box–sized package was too small for supplies. Besides, who would send a child to bring it?

I handed him a piece of chocolate cream candy. The boy grinned and skipped out the door.

Using a pair of scissors, I cut into the box. Nestled inside sat another smaller replica of the one I'd opened. I smiled. Ethan must be up to his pranks.

Loving surprises, I ripped into the second box. My hand paused in midair. I gasped and dropped the container.

In the center of a pile of chocolate that looked like it had been melted and reset, lay a dead rat.

15

Now we'll have the health department here. I would need to sanitize the entire store with about a million gallons of bleach.

Get control of yourself, Summer. Don't let Aunt Eunice see it. She'll freak.

I slapped the box closed before she peeked over my shoulder, tucked it under my arm, and sprinted for the bathroom. My first instinct was to throw it away, but I knew I needed the dead animal as evidence to prove my case to Joe.

"Summer?"

I kicked the door closed. "Be right out." The tiny room contained a pedestal sink and a toilet. I stuffed the box behind the plumbing, flushed, then washed my hands. With a deep breath, I opened the door.

Aunt Eunice waited, arms crossed and foot tapping. "What are you doing?"

"Uh, using the restroom?"

"Fastest time ever recorded if you did. What was in the box?"

"Nothing." Well, the first box *was* empty, kind

of, except for the thing inside. I glanced to where the outward packaging still rested on the counter.

"Summer, you're a terrible liar." She pushed me out of the way and stepped into the small space.

I closed my eyes and waited. Before I counted to five, my aunt screamed and dashed back out.

"I tried to hide it from you."

The odor of burnt peanuts permeated the candy store. "The brittle!" Grabbing a hot pad from a nearby shelf, I darted to save my candy. The mixture had moved past the greenish tinge of perfectly cooked peanut brittle to the dark brown of scorched nuts. This obviously wasn't a candy making day. I turned off the gas and started scooping for the second time.

"I'm calling Joe. This is getting out of hand." Aunt Eunice marched to the phone hanging on the wall, punched in some numbers, then demanded to speak with her nephew. After disconnecting, she turned to me. "He's on his way. Said not to do anything with the box. He also said not to touch it. He isn't talking about the rat, is he? He doesn't think we'd actually touch that thing, does he?"

I shook my head. "No, I'm sure it's the box he means."

Joe would be furious to know I'd carried then tucked the offending item behind the toilet. It wouldn't help that Aunt Eunice's fingerprints were also on it. We couldn't leave it out front for a customer to see. My throat constricted at the thought of Ethan's reaction. How much could he take and still be supportive?

Maybe things *were* getting dangerous, but I

could handle it. The few times I'd gone to my self-defense classes would help. I could do a roundhouse kick with the best of them.

Maybe. If I had to.

I poured boiling water over the sticky mess on the sides of the vat, washing the gunk to the bottom. After covering the congealed mess, I lit the fire to steam the last of it from the copper sides. If only life were that easy. Light a fire, and steam away the hardest part.

The bell over the door jingled. Joe stormed in. Aunt Eunice bustled to meet him. I stayed right where I was.

"Joe, we got us a chocolate-covered crime. Right in there behind the toilet." Perfect. After getting over her fear of the

dead rodent, Aunt Eunice grew witty.

Joe's eyebrows rose so high that if he'd had bangs, they would have disappeared. "You said you received a threatening package. What's it doing in the bathroom?"

My aunt planted her fists on her hips. "Summer put it there. Tried to hide it from me so I'd find it and be surprised. I almost had a heart attack."

"I did not. I wanted to keep you from finding it and freaking out. My heart was in the right place." Where did the ideas in my aunt's head come from?

"Who delivered it?" Joe stepped past us and into the bathroom. He nudged the box with his toe.

"The rat's dead, Joe. It won't hurt you. Some little boy brought it in." I lifted the package and thrust it toward him. "Here. Other than mine and Aunt Eunice's fingerprints, it ought to be clean."

"A rat?" He drew back like it would bite him.

What a baby! I pushed the box into his chest. Joe put his hands up. So much for my not touching it anymore. "Didn't Aunt Eunice tell you what had been delivered?"

Exaggerating my movements, I stomped to where we kept our plastic garbage bags, ripped one from the roll, dropped the disgusting rat's coffin inside, then handed it to my cousin. "Better?" And him a big cop with a gun.

Joe grimaced and took the bag. "Did you question the boy? What did he look like?"

"Question him? Why? He delivered a package. There wasn't a reason to suspect anything. He was dark haired, skinny; he looked like any other little boy." I folded my arms and grinned, thoroughly enjoying my cousin's discomfort.

He grabbed a dish towel and wiped perspiration from his forehead. "Did you try chasing him down?"

"No, I tried hiding the rat from my aunt." Wasn't he listening?

"Is there anyone who would gain from threatening you?"

He had to be kidding. I mentally counted off the names. "Seven that I can think of. All names in Mae Belle's book. All people I've questioned. Most of whom have threatened me in one way or another and told me to keep my nose out of things. *Now* are you going to take me seriously?"

"Yes, he is. A dead rat is not to be taken lightly." Aunt Eunice shoved against Joe's back. "Take that disgusting thing out back. You can finish questioning Summer outside."

***

"You should have seen the way Joe held that bagged rat away from him, using just his fingertips. Hilarious." Aunt Eunice set a plate of spaghetti in front of Uncle Roy. I smiled, thinking of how she'd conveniently forgotten her own show of hysterics upon sight of the rodent.

Uncle Roy dumped Parmesan cheese on his noodles. "I don't like the direction this is heading, Summer. You'd think you would have learned from the last two escapades you had."

By escapades, I assumed he meant mysteries. "I promised Mae Belle I'd find out who killed her. I plan on keeping that promise. If you're scared, go visit Aunt Claudia."

Uncle Roy speared a meatball with unnecessary force. "Who said anything about being scared? And don't think you can just run me out of my own house." His hand paused. "Okay, it's your house, but I've lived here for years. I figure I can call it my house if I want."

The pasta made it to his mouth. He chewed, his gaze settled on me. "I just don't want anything to happen to my little girl. You can't be lucky forever."

"That's what people keep telling me." I twirled a forkful of pasta. "But I figure God overrules any amount of luck." Although it would be nice if someone came along to help. Someone I could brainstorm with.

Aunt Eunice is afraid of getting arrested again, and April is too occupied with Joe. Plus, she's a sissy. Ethan's busy with the high school, and I really need to start planning my wedding."

Listing the reasons no one could be my sidekick depressed me. The carnival mystery had been so much more fun with Ethan going on stakeouts with me. Then spending the night in jail with Aunt Eunice had been. . .interesting. Kind of. At least different. I shrugged and took a bite of spaghetti.

"Don't forget we're getting low on products at the store." Aunt Eunice swirled her noodles in the sauce.

"Thanks for reminding me." I let my fork clatter to the plate.

Uncle Roy leaned across and put a hand over mine. "Sweetie, you don't have to do this. Joe will find Mae Belle's killer. You just focus on getting married."

"I promised."

He straightened. "Don't get me wrong, but Mae Belle isn't around to collect."

"Let your 'yes,' be 'yes' and your 'no,' 'no.' Anything else is of the devil. Isn't that what the Bible says?"

Uncle Roy opened his mouth to respond and closed it instead. He pursed his lips then said, "Can't argue with that. Eunice, help the girl on her quest."

The ringing of the doorbell, and Truly's shrill barking, saved her from answering. Uncle Roy pushed back his chair. "I'll get it. We ain't expecting anyone, are we?"

He returned in seconds, his face pale.

"Y'all need to come look. Seems someone has

left Summer another gift."

We rose and followed him to the front porch. My heart lodged in my throat. What would it be now? A finger, another rat, a severed head? I shook my head to stop my overactive imagination and glanced at my feet.

In a wire animal carrier, curled into a ball, slept a sleek black-and-white kitten. A note taped to the front read, "To go along with the rat."

"At least the cat ain't dead." Uncle Roy lifted the cage. "What are we going to do with this little thing? Truly won't be very happy to have a feline as company."

"She'll get used to it." My heart fell back into place at the sight of the sleeping kitten. But why would someone leave a dead rat, then a live cat? The three of us went back inside, taking the cage with us. Now, who did I know who had cats? Just about every neighbor within a five-mile radius.

We hadn't made it to the kitchen before the doorbell rang again. "I'll get it!" I darted toward the door and peered out the window.

Uh-oh. Ethan stood outside, arms crossed. He wasn't smiling.

124

16

Hi, Ethan." I wrapped my arms around his neck and kissed him. He lifted me off my feet. After putting me down, he took my hand and led me to the porch swing.

Smooth-talking man. He let me get comfortable before he spoke. "Joe called me this afternoon. Seems you got an interesting gift."

"Two, actually. One's in the house."

"You have another dead rat inside?" He stiffened.

I giggled. "No, a cute little tuxedo kitten. The note said he went with the rat, but that's obviously a joke."

"I want you to stop now." Ethan turned me to face him. "I've tried to be supportive. I know how much you enjoy doing this, but. . ."

"What? You won't marry me?" My throat clogged. My greatest fear was about to come true.

"Nothing could make me not marry you. Don't you know me better than that?"

"Aunt Eunice told me I needed to get it out of

my system before our wedding."

"That would be nice." He ran a hand through his hair. "What am I saying? It won't make any difference. Now or then. The fact is—this is getting too dangerous." He groaned and leaned his head back, closing his eyes.

He sighed and stared at me. "You're going to be the death of me, Summer. I love you, very much. The thought of losing you. . .almost stops my heart, it's so intense."

God hadn't created a more special man. And he was all mine. I clasped a hand to my chest to hold my heart inside. "Help me. You enjoyed it during the fair. That was only a month ago. Surely the excitement hasn't worn off yet."

I smoothed the strands sticking up on his head. Had it really been such a short amount of time? Once Ethan had mentioned getting married in the spring, I'd phoned my cousin right away.

He stilled my hands. "I can't. Not with school and coaching the football team. Unless you wait until the weekends to follow your leads. I'm also going to talk with Mason White. See why he followed you today."

"You believe me?"

"We'll wait and see what he says. He's having a party Friday night, and surprisingly we're invited." Ethan pulled an envelope from the pocket of his jeans and handed it to me. It was an embossed invitation. "This must be your doing."

"One of those murder-mystery nights?" I'd always wanted to go to one of those. "Who am I going to be?"

"We're going as Dan and Pat Sheraton. A well-to-do elderly couple. Dress the part, and try to have fun." He stood and bent to kiss me. "I'll call you tomorrow. I love you. Please, be careful."

"I love you." My mind raced as he strolled to his truck, then turned to wave.

A mystery party would be the perfect opportunity to snoop. It'd be expected, right? I blew Ethan a kiss and went inside.

Why would Mason invite us to his party? Ethan didn't know him, beyond a remote acquaintance, and all I'd succeeded in doing was to annoy the man.

I went in search of my new pet. Aunt Eunice had opened the kitty carrier, and I found the little ball of fluff sleeping in the trash can next to the dryer. He'd made his bed among the dryer sheets and lint. "Okay, little guy. Your name is going to be Trashcan."

I lifted him, noting the bell hanging from his collar didn't jingle. I set the kitten on the washing machine and unhooked the bell. Stuffed inside was a tiny, rolled slip of paper.

A rat in chocolate and a kitten with a bell that doesn't work.

That's it? It didn't make any sense. I leaned against the washing machine and read it again. What did the sender want to tell me? Nothing or just part of the game?

I carried the note to the kitchen where Aunt Eunice finished the last of the dishes. "Here. Read this." She dried her hands on her apron. "This is silly. What's it got to do with anything?"

I shrugged. "Someone is having a lot of fun at my expense."

"Who do we know who has a cat?"

"Everyone?"

"Okay, wisecracker." Still clutching the paper, Aunt Eunice sat in the closest chair. "A rat in chocolate and a kitten with a bell that doesn't work. What's next, a dog without a bark?" She snorted.

"Very funny." I snatched the note from her hand. "Ethan and I are going to a party at Mason White's on Friday. I'm going to do some snooping that doesn't have anything to do with the mystery game Mason's hosting."

"You think he sent the note?"

"I don't know. But he *has* threatened me, he *likes* to play games, and this will be the perfect opportunity."

"Should we call Joe? Now that we've probably smudged any fingerprints that might have been on it."

Why didn't I think of those things? I was the detective.

"I'll call him right now and tell him what it says." I grabbed the wall phone and stretched the cord across the kitchen until I could sit across from my aunt. Why wouldn't they let me put a cordless phone in this room?

"Hey, Joe."

"Yep. What did you do now?"

"What makes you think I did anything?" Really.

"Uh-huh."

"You're just full of conversation, aren't you? I was petting Trashcan, the new kitten. . ."

"When did you get a kitten?"

"Someone dropped it off on our porch. Anyway. . ."

"What do you mean 'dropped it off'?"

I sighed. "I'm trying to tell you. If you'd stop interrupting me. Anyway, I noticed his bell didn't ring. So, I investigated. There was a note inside where that little dinger thing is supposed to be." I read him the note. "What do you think it means?"

"Who else have you shown it to?"

"Aunt Eunice. We both touched it. Do you want it, since our fingerprints are all over it?"

"Not tonight. Hang on to it, and give it to me tomorrow." His sigh vibrated over the airwaves. "I don't know what it means. Maybe nothing. Maybe it's a clue, and we're missing something. What kind of paper is it written on?"

"It looks like someone tore off a corner of a sheet of copy paper and printed, really small, with a pencil. Whoever wrote it has good handwriting. Does that mean it's from a woman?" Clue number one.

"Not necessarily. Plenty of men have excellent penmanship."

There was a long pause. "Hello?" Joe was so quiet I thought he'd hung up. "Anyone there?"

"Just thinking. I don't like this, cousin. Not a bit. Back off and be careful." Click.

Clue shot down like the Red Baron's plane. I decided to head back to A Dream Wedding tomorrow and see whether

or not I could find something with Sherry's handwriting. Or Renee Richards's. Regardless of what Joe thought, I'd start with my female suspects.

After a quick game of hide–and-seek with Truly, I spent the rest of the evening trying to make my print very tiny. When I'd finished, the words, minus my curly letters, could've been written by anyone. I consoled myself with the fact not everyone had as expressive writing as I did.

***

The dark windows of A Dream Wedding set a melancholy mood as I entered through the front door. I said a prayer of thanks that no crime-scene tape circled the store. It wasn't until I stepped about ten paces in that I realized the store should have been locked up tight.

"Hello?" I flicked on the light switch. "Anybody here?"

I dug through my purse and pulled out my cell phone, clutching it like a weapon. A rustling noise from the back lured me like a sweet tooth after a lollipop. I flipped light switches as I passed.

Sherry's broad behind greeted me from a storage closet. She shrieked when I called her name and fell forward. Brooms and mops crashed to the floor with her.

"What are you doing here?" She struggled to her feet.

"I could ask you the same question." I dropped my phone back in its case. "Keeping the business going without Mae

Belle?"

"No." She straightened her blouse. "I left something, and I've come back to get it."

"You have a key?"

"Yes. I often worked longer hours than she did. Mae Belle trusted me." Sherry pushed past me and closed the closet door.

What could she have lost in a supply closet? I'd be back at another time to search more thoroughly. "I'm just here to get the notes Mae Belle took for my wedding. I'll be finished in a jiffy." My spine tingled as I marched away from her, expecting at any moment to have something sticking out of my back.

The pink and white rug that once spread beneath the desk had been removed. Other than black powder over every available surface, the room looked the way it had when I'd found Mae Belle.

I set my purse on the cleanest corner of the desk and opened the closest file drawer. Not much in there.

I grabbed the handful of files and riffled through them. There had to be something here with handwriting that didn't belong to my cousin.

One of those lethal, pointy note holders held many slips of messages. I grabbed them, pricking my finger in the process. Sherry's chicken scratch could in no way match the note attached around Trashcan's neck. I continued my search.

"What are you doing?" Sherry's screech sent me flying back in my chair.

"I told you. Looking for my file." My heart thudded.

She reminded me of an outraged, out-of-shape Amazon warrior. "What are *you* looking for? Maybe I'll find it." She grabbed the messages from my hand. "Mae Belle hadn't had time to make you a file yet."

She stalked to the cabinet, yanked the files from the desk, and tossed them back in the drawer. "Any notes she took would be here." I scooted back as quickly as possible to avoid being rammed in the gut by the desk drawer.

Sherry tossed a fluorescent yellow folder in front of me. "There you go. Next time, ask."

When I stepped outside into the late September sunshine, I realized Sherry hadn't answered my question.

17

Aunt Eunice arrived at work to the sight of me with pastel-colored papers spread across the marble slab in the back room. Most of the notes had nothing to do with my wedding. The colors were wrong, the food something I'd never choose, and who wanted carnations in their wedding bouquet?

I fought the urge to swipe everything to the floor. No wonder Mae Belle left a long line of disgruntled customers. She didn't pay attention to what they wanted.

"What's up?" Aunt Eunice lifted a page.

"These are supposed to be Mae Belle's notes for my wedding. Nothing's right."

I scooped the papers back in a pile. Good thing I'd kept my own set of notes in my tote bag. My glance fell on a circled letter within the name of a flower. Then another in the description of a wedding dress. A word within the ingredients of a cake.

I fanned through the sheets. "Look at these words."

"What do you think it means?"

"I think Mae Belle got my notes wrong on purpose. Get me a pencil." I spread the pages in a line, wishing I'd kept them in order. I scribbled the circled letters and words, holding my breath. If my hunch proved true, the puzzle Mae Belle left behind might show the identity of her killer.

I stared at the confusing jargon in front of me. This could take forever.

Circled words. Circled letters. I hated word games. "Aunt Eunice, can you help me?"

"Do you realize how many messages we could make with this list?"

"That's why I need your help." I tossed the pencil down. "Two heads are better than one."

"Fine." She picked up the pencil. "Let's count the letters. How many *A*s are there?"

"One."

"Great. *B*s?" And so on we went until I grew more confused than ever.

"There are six *S*s. Let's assume the message begins with your name. Also, she's given us some words to work with— *something, cushions, sofa,* and *happen.*"

"Some of the *S*s you asked for are in those words."

"Doesn't matter." Aunt Eunice chewed the end of the pencil. Whenever I tried to volunteer an idea, she shushed me.

Two hours later, with me bored out of my mind, she grinned. "Solved it."

She handed the message to me. *Summer, if something should happen to me, look in the cushions of my red and white sofa. M.B.*

I frowned. "How do you know this is what it says?"

"It makes sense. Look at the letters that are left after you use the words. There are only so many possibilities. You just try them all until you hit on something. And Mae Belle did have a red and white sofa."

Horror. We'd donated it after cleaning out her apartment.

I grabbed my purse. "Let's go. Hopefully, Secondhand Bart still has that monstrosity in his store."

We hung out a Be Back Soon sign and hopped in the car. Each mile nearer to the resale shop brought me that much closer to solving Mae Belle's murder. She wouldn't have taken the time to leave me a message if it weren't to tell me something important.

Worse, she probably suspected something might happen to her and needed to tell someone about it in secret. Goose pimples prickled my flesh.

"Slow down, Summer." Aunt Eunice clutched her purse to her stomach.

I glanced at the speedometer. Seventy! I eased my foot off the pedal. "Sorry. We could have this case solved by tonight, Aunt Eunice. Imagine." Then I could get back to planning my wedding.

"Don't jump the gun. Mae Belle had a tendency to be a little wacky. Could be a wild-goose chase. Why didn't she just leave the clue in her office? Or a safety deposit box? Or mail it? Now that's a concept."

"I don't know. One thing at a time. I'm just

hoping the sofa is still with Bart." My nerves twitched like live wires by the time we arrived at the consignment shop.

Right away, my gaze landed on Mae Belle's seven-foot sofa stuffed in a back corner. *Thank You, God.* I marched over, lifted a cushion, and unzipped the cover.

"Excuse me?" Bart's paunch blocked my view. A stain in the shape of Texas stretched across his belly. "May I help you?"

"I need to look inside these cushions." I shoved my hand beneath the cotton fabric feeling nothing but rough foam. I tossed the cushion and grabbed another.

Bart snatched it from my hands and leaned over me. I glanced up into a ruddy face with a bulbous nose and flashing green eyes. "Stop."

I tried standing, bounced off his gut, and landed back where I'd started. I could've asked him to move, but his expression told me my request wouldn't be well received. I kept my gaze focused on his stomach. The stain danced as he breathed.

"I'm sorry, Bart, but we donated this sofa to you, and we left something in one of the cushions."

"I'm not Bart, and anything left is now mine."

"Then let me speak to Bart."

"There isn't a Bart." He spoke slowly and distinctly like he thought I'd have trouble understanding.

"How much?" Aunt Eunice stepped forward. "We'll buy the sofa."

"Aunt Eunice!"

Non-Bart backed up and grinned. "Seventy-five

dollars."

"Sold." Aunt Eunice wrote him a check while I resumed my digging.

Aha! Deep in one of the corners, I found a folded triangle of paper. "Got it!"

"Great." Aunt Eunice turned back to Non-Bart. "I'm now re-donating the sofa and would like a receipt for tax purposes."

I smiled. Good ole' Aunt Eunice. The woman thought of everything. I fairly skipped to my car, the triangle clutched in my fist like a prize.

"Well, let's see it." Aunt Eunice slid into the front seat. "I've got a headache from breaking the code. Don't keep me waiting."

I unfolded the paper and groaned. Water stains marred the words. What had Non-Bart done? Cleaned the sofa? I'd need a brighter light than the failing sun to be able to make anything out.

"It looks like a list." Aunt Eunice peered at the paper as I drove. "No, a list of thoughts—like clues. *Computer, scam, money.* . .I can't make out the rest."

"Mae Belle knew something about someone. But what? This whole thing is driving me crazy."

"We're getting closer all the time. Almost as close as you are to that car." My aunt clutched the dashboard.

My tires screeched as I slammed on the brakes. Aunt Eunice's purse hit the floor between her feet. My heart lodged in my throat. The driver of the Cadillac sent me an obscene gesture through his rearview mirror. I waved apologetically in return and willed my pulse to slow.

"Well, that was fun." Aunt Eunice retrieved her spilled belongings and straightened. "Best I can figure out from Mae Belle's waterlogged clues is that someone was a victim of a computer scam. And since most people nowadays have a computer, it could be anyone."

I pressed the accelerator. "Mae Belle figured out who was scamming whom, and the rest is history."

But where did I go from here? How many people in Mountain Shadows would fall for a computer scam? We might be country, but we weren't stupid. But were any of us capable of sticking a letter opener in Mae Belle's back? I shook my head. No, the wielder of the deadly weapon must be the person responsible for the scam.

I'd really been hoping to find out whose handwriting matched the note on Trashcan's collar. How could I get a peek at Renee's handwriting? Her printing, not cursive.

"You're speeding again." Aunt Eunice tightened her seat belt.

"Sorry." I needed to get back into A Dream Wedding. There had to be something left from Mae Belle's planning of Renee's birthday party.

I'd go tonight. I pressed harder on the gas pedal.

18

Dressed in black jeans and a turtleneck sweater, I pulled a knit cap over my head. I didn't need my hair shining like a red-light special announcing to the world I snooped through A Dream Wedding after hours. I grabbed my bag of investigating tools and sneaked downstairs, avoiding where the floor creaked.

"Where are you going?"

I shrieked and whirled. Aunt Eunice stepped around the corner. "How did you know I was going anywhere?"

"These walls are thin, Summer. I heard you getting dressed. It's a good thing your uncle sleeps like the dead, or you wouldn't be going anywhere."

"I'm going to Mae Belle's shop. I didn't have time to search thoroughly earlier."

"I'm going with you." Aunt Eunice moved into the glow from the hall night-light also dressed in dark colors. "I knew you were up to something. I got ready and waited."

I couldn't help but grin. "Sneaky woman. You do realize we might get into trouble?"

"Bring it on, honey." She giggled and locked the door behind us. "This detective stuff gets under your skin, doesn't it? Burrows in just like a chigger."

"Ethan told me to buy bug spray to take care of the mystery problem. It *is* kind of like an insect that digs in and doesn't let go."

The closer we got to A Dream Wedding, the sillier we became until we snorted with laughter. My eyes watered. The promise of adventure ensnared us with its euphoria. I pulled into the alley behind the store and cut the lights.

A street lamp highlighted the door like a portal. I grabbed my bag, exited the car, then stood staring at the building.

The alley didn't afford any glimpse inside. My heart skipped a beat. What if someone waited, lurking in the shadows, with the evil intent of finishing me off? I choked back a scream when Aunt Eunice clapped me on the shoulder.

"Come on. I've got a key. Claudia gave it to me." She marched forward and unlocked the door. "I'll turn on the lights."

"No, I don't want anyone to know we're here this late. Too many questions." Inside, I flicked on my nifty little flashlight. "I'm looking for anything that matches the handwriting on this." I handed her the note from Trashcan's collar.

"Weren't you supposed to turn this over to Joe?"

"Haven't had the chance. He knows where it is if he wants it." I ran the light beam over the storage room. "My guess is that one of Mae Belle's previous clients left their signature, notes, something behind. And whatever it is, it matches this print. I'm going through her office again. You check in front behind the counter."

Aunt Eunice pulled a flashlight from under her sweatshirt. "I came prepared." She brandished it like a warrior's sword and stalked away, shining the light from one corner of the store to the other.

My gaze fell on the plate glass window that graced the front of the building. "Stop flashing that light around. You're announcing to the whole town that we're in here."

"Okeydoke."

I headed to my destination, pulled the blinds closed on the office window, then turned on the light. I plopped my bag on the desk and my bottom in Mae Belle's office chair.

She'd spent her inheritance well. The chair cushioned me, folding me in leather softness. With a sigh, I glanced around. I'd checked the file cabinet already. Where else could my scatterbrained cousin have stashed notes?

A Rolodex caught my attention, and I flipped through the few cards with names and numbers. Every name on my suspect list was in there. I grabbed an empty card and scribbled down the information. Bangs and thuds came from the front of the store.

"Aunt Eunice?" I dropped the card in my bag.

"I'm all right. Just looking! Knocked over some ugly statue thing. Its head fell off."

I gazed around the room. For something so gaudily decorated, Mae Belle had kept it impossibly neat. Surely one of her clients had written down something she'd kept.

"Woo-hoo! Found something."

Great. I leaped to my feet and sprinted to join my aunt.

She handed me a slip of pink paper. "Here."

Written in impossibly small and precise print was a note detailing the time and place of Renee Richards's birthday party, now passed. My hunch was correct. In some way, Renee was involved in Mae Belle's death.

The store lit up with a flash of bright light. I squinted against the glare and stumbled backward. "You in the store!

Come out with your hands up."

Horror. I grabbed Aunt Eunice's hand and dragged her with me toward the alley.

"We're going to jail. We're going to jail." Her chants were interspersed with gasps for air. "Oh Lord, not again."

I ducked into Mae Belle's office, grabbed my bag, then whirled to yank open the back door. "Come on." I glanced back at my aunt, turned to dart out the door, and ran into a navy-covered chest. The impact knocked me back.

My head banged the brick wall behind me. Breath left me.

"When we got the call about lights, why did I suspect you?" Joe stood with his feet firmly planted even after I plowed into him. I struggled to stand despite the colorful stars blinking in front of my eyes. "And how did I know you'd try to run out the back?"

"Please, Joe, have mercy." Aunt Eunice folded her hands as if in prayer. "It was Summer's idea. Please don't take us back to jail."

He pushed her hands down. "I'm not taking you to jail, but the two of you had better have found something interesting."

"Why aren't you upset?" This didn't seem like the Joe I'd grown up with. This one sported a grin, like he'd caught us in a joke. Okay, maybe he did resemble the younger Joe, definitely not the stern Big Cop-Man I called him behind his back.

"I heard in a roundabout way, you know how that lawyer Biggs can't keep his mouth shut, that Mae Belle left the business to you, dear cousin. So officially, you weren't trespassing."

A Dream Wedding belonged to me? Aunt Claudia would have a coronary. What would I do with it? The candy store took up most of my time as it was. "Then why the theatrics? You practically scared us to death." I shoved his shoulder.

"With all the extra work you cause me, I'm entitled to a little fun. What did you find?"

I pulled the note from the cat's collar out of my pocket. "Here's what Trashcan wore around his neck, and here is a note with handwriting that matches." I raised my eyebrows waiting for him to say, "well done."

"Humph."

"That's all you have to say? I'm going to question Renee, somehow, tomorrow night at Mason's party. I'm sure she'll be going. They appear to be quite chummy."

"April and I are invited, too. But let me do the

questioning. You don't have the authority. I questioned Mason about following you. He said he was just having a little fun because you take your detecting so seriously. Seemed to be telling the truth." Joe waved the paper at me. "I'm sure this is the same thing. Mason and Renee having a little fun at your expense. I'll talk to them."

I folded my arms and gave my tongue free rein. "I read somewhere that the male—whatever it is that makes a man male, a chromosome or something—is damaged when entering the woman's uterus. Brain damaged. Basically, that makes you inferior to women, seeing as how we remain undamaged throughout the cycle of conception."

Grabbing Aunt Eunice's arm, I marched away from my wide-eyed cousin and slid behind the wheel of my car. "I'd say that gives me plenty of authority," I muttered.

"Is that true?" Aunt Eunice clicked her seat belt.

"I did read it somewhere. I just can't tell you where. And I'm not positive I got the facts right, but I got my point across." I squealed tires out of the alley.

"I can't wait to inform your uncle Roy the next time he's acting dense."

She'd get her chance pretty quick. Uncle Roy sat in a wicker rocking chair on the front porch, trusty rifle cradled in his arms when we pulled into the driveway.

I cut the engine. "You didn't tell him you were leaving, did you?"

She shoved open her door. "He wouldn't have

let either of us go." She glanced at her watch. "Especially at one o'clock in the morning."

"Did Joe find you?" Uncle Roy kept rocking.

"You called him?" Aunt Eunice crunched across the gravel and stood in front of the porch. She proceeded to spout off the newest bit of trivia I'd taught her. The more I thought of it, the more convinced I became that maybe I'd heard the information from a comedian. I shrugged and continued to watch the drama before me.

"Are you sassing me, Eunice? Of course I called him. You were missing."

Uh-oh. I squeezed past what promised to be a full-scale marital war.

"Summer." *Horror.* Ethan marched from the kitchen with two cans of soda clutched in his hands. "Where have you been?"

19

After a short lecture last night about disappearing without telling Ethan or Uncle Roy where I'd gone, we'd discussed our disguises for the party. He'd forgiven me, some, when he realized I hadn't gone alone. He wasn't thrilled, but not angry either.

Ethan and I had gone to a used-clothing store and bought an old dress for me and a suit for him. I pulled a comb through my hair and tugged on a short gray wig, struggling to get my curls to stay under the tight headpiece. I smoothed the skirt of my costume.

The polka-dot dress hung on me like a flour sack. It's a wonder I was leaving the house dressed like this. I stuck my arms through a yellow sweater and rushed downstairs to join Ethan.

He laughed. "This is what you'll look like as an old lady? I might have to rethink getting married." He'd powdered his hair. The suit he wore had obviously been made for a man larger around the middle than my buff country boy. The pants bunched beneath a tightly cinched belt, giving

Ethan the illusion of a paunch.

I poked his stomach with my finger. "Don't laugh, mister. All you need to complete your outfit is a cane."

Ethan pulled an aluminum cane from around the hall corner and twirled it. His eyes twinkled with humor. "Anything else?"

"I think that's it." I grinned and linked my arm in his.

Mason's renovated plantation home glowed like a tiered birthday cake. Couples strolled across manicured lawns in costumes portraying all walks of life. I couldn't help but wonder how the man thought he could throw a murder-mystery party with this many people. There had to be around fifteen couples. How could anyone keep anything straight?

We declined the glass of wine offered at the door and let a young woman dressed as a maid usher us into a large living room.

Mason stood near a massive brick fireplace, depicting a man of leisure in khaki pants and navy blazer. "Welcome to my party. I'm playing myself, Mason White." He lifted his goblet in a toast.

"Tonight's mystery has been specially engineered just for me and my guests. Enjoy, mingle, and search for clues. Hidden around my home are many weapons, slips of paper, and other paraphernalia pertaining to a crime. The victim is the pretty young thing who answered the door.

"Her body now lies on the chaise lounge in the study. Others of you may end up disappearing or finding yourselves murdered. You'll know if it happens, so keep your wits about you.

"Dinner is buffet style in the dining room. Have fun! And may the best sleuth remain standing."

A bit odd, but I couldn't help the surge of adrenaline coursing through me at the thought of an innocent night of fun doing what I enjoyed—snooping.

I gripped Ethan's hand. "Let's take a look at the body. That's the best starting point."

He laughed. "A bit macabre, but okay."

The "victim" flopped back, closed her eyes, and threw an arm across her face, leaving the other one to dangle from the chaise when we strode into the room. An empty wineglass lay on the floor. Red liquid stained the carpet.

"Poison." I nudged the goblet with my foot. "Now, we need a motive and a suspect. Which means"—I wiggled my eyebrows at Ethan—"we get to snoop around Mason's house."

"Only pertaining to the game, Summer. And what makes you so sure it's poison?"

"Elementary, my dear Watson. There's no blood, no ligature markings around the neck, no bump on the head. This will be so much fun." Hooking my arm through his, I led Ethan from the room. "Where do you want to start?"

"The dining room? I'm starved. Maybe we can eavesdrop while loading our plates."

It didn't take much of our mingling to discover the other guests all had scripts and played their characters to the hilt. Had Ethan and I been a last-minute addition to the guest list?

I speared Mason with my gaze. He grinned his

shark smile from across the room and saluted me.

"Ethan?"

"Yeah?" He popped a stuffed mushroom into his mouth.

"Did Mason mention why he didn't give us scripts? Backgrounds for our characters? Alibis?"

Ethan wiped his mouth with a monogrammed napkin. "Said he invited us at the last minute. He also said it gave us an advantage. Meaning, we're definitely not the murderer. We get to fly by the seat of our pants, making up our alibis and stories as we go. It's a bit suspicious, but I thought we'd play along with his little game. And I don't mean the murder mystery.

"I'll admit it. Something isn't right with our host. But hear me—you aren't going anywhere unless I'm right beside you."

I grinned. I knew he'd see it my way. Besides, snooping was more fun when he joined in. "There's Joe and April." I waved my hand to get their attention.

"Did you hear a word I said?" Ethan frowned.

"Every bit."

"Hey, Summer. Seen the body yet?" April gave her brother a hug. "The girl isn't that good. She was sitting up when we went in."

"Did ya'll get scripts?"

"Yeah. Joe's a detective, and I'm his flapper girlfriend. Like the dress?"

Great. She got to come as a cute young thing in a black sequined dress while I was an old lady. "We didn't get anything."

At least I'm here. Forgive me, Lord, for being

envious.

"Well, time to go nose around. See ya later."

Joe leaned closer to Ethan. "I hope she's talking about the game."

"Of sorts." Ethan handed his plate to a passing waiter. "I'll keep her out of trouble." He winked and steered me toward the hall. "Who do you want to question first?"

I spotted Renee slipping past Mason, one manicured claw brushing across his back as she passed. "Her." We followed her outside to the patio.

Renee leaned against the banister, letting her head fall back. Her long hair blew in the slight breeze. She bent one knee, balancing her foot against the rails.

"Hello, Renee. Thanks for the kitten." I tried positioning my body into the same glamorous pose. Somehow, I figured the costume detracted from the appearance I wanted to give, and I straightened.

"Summer. Ethan." Her voice fairly purred when she said his name. "Y'all having fun? And you're welcome about the kitten. I don't care how you found out I left it. Mason and I are just playing with you. You take this detective stuff so seriously."

Very funny. "What about the rat?"

She laughed. "Mason's idea. Clever, wasn't it?"

"It was all just a game?" *Great.* I felt like a dodo head for thinking the rat and the kitten were somehow connected with my cousin's murder.

Renee nodded. "We wanted to see how long it would take you to figure it out. Especially with the silly clue left in the cat's collar. You solved it quickly. I'm impressed."

"Where were you the night Mae Belle died?"

"Summer, sweetie, you've got the wrong body. Stay in the game." She turned to look at me. "If I remember my notes, I was upstairs taking a nap, alone, when Mimi the maid was killed. I don't have an alibi, but my hobby is botany. Have you found out what the poor girl was poisoned with?"

I mentally slapped myself in the head. I'd stopped at the murder weapon. Maybe if I actually asked questions pertaining to the game, I could slip real investigative questions in by surprise. Trip up my suspect. I grabbed Ethan's hand.

"Let's investigate the body and the room further."

The victim plopped back to her prone position when we entered. Mason should've done a better job of choosing his victim. If she'd move around with people searching the room, the girl didn't lend much to the illusion. Another couple prowled the room peeking beneath cushions and behind curtains. If they hadn't found anything, I wouldn't waste my time retracing their steps.

I frowned at the "actress" and headed for the desk while directing Ethan toward the rows of bookshelves. The top middle drawer revealed an ornate letter opener with, were those real gemstones? Stamps, paper clips, a gold pen, a pair of pointy scissors, and a rope.

I giggled. All I needed was a wrench and lead pipe.

Ethan held up a candlestick. "I feel like we're playing the board game Clue."

I slammed the drawer closed. "Nothing in here.

Let's try the bathroom."

We passed a giggling April and Joe snuggling on a vacant bench in the hall. I guessed my cousin enjoyed his rare time out of uniform.

"Y'all found any clues yet?"

April stared at me. "Any what?"

"Exactly." I grinned at Ethan and pulled him along behind me. "Let's solve this pretend mystery and move on to the real one."

A group of guests crowded around Mason who stood near the bathroom with his arm slung around Renee's shoulders. "Has everyone here met the beautiful lady, Bella Donna?"

Renee definitely got a better name and outfit than I'd received. I scowled in her direction and pushed past everyone until I practically fell through the throng and into the restroom. Ethan's arm around my waist prevented me from hitting the tile floor on my knees. Steadied, I opened the medicine cabinet.

"Cute." I withdrew a prescription bottle covered with a slip of paper on which someone had drawn a skull and written the word *belladonna*. Belladonna?

"Ethan, I've solved it. Simple, really. I would've loved more of a challenge, but now we can get on with the real thing."

Which I could guarantee wouldn't be as easy to solve.

Mason and Renee had disappeared by the time we forced our way through the people still standing outside the restroom. I informed April and Joe I'd solved the case as we marched past them. At least they'd risen from the bench in the time we'd been gone. Why come to the party if they were going to stay to themselves the whole time?

"Which case?" Joe lowered his brows.

"The game, silly." Really, the man could be so dense.

"Tell us how it was done!" April skipped beside me, leaving Joe to walk with Ethan.

"No. Joe's a cop. If y'all had been the slightest bit interested, you'd have solved it an hour ago."

"Come on. He doesn't get a lot of time off. We wanted to make the most of it." She glanced over her shoulder.

"You can come with me when I talk to Renee."

A scream ripped down the hall.

20

Ethan and Joe sprinted past April and me. We followed at a fast walk. April clutched my arm like the scaredy-cat she'd proven to be, and slowed me down. I tried shrugging her off to move faster, but she dug her claws in deeper. For your typical bouncy blond, she showed signs of being a party pooper.

"Do you think it's part of the game?" Her voice squeaked despite the whisper.

"Maybe. If you'd loosen your grip, we could go see."

"What if it isn't?" She squealed.

I shook my arm. "Mason said others would disappear or be murdered. The party's been pretty lame so far. Maybe he's shaking things up."

She released her viselike hold. "I'd forgotten. How silly of me. This might be fun."

Lord, if I get as dizzy headed as my friend, go ahead and fry me with a bolt of lightning. Ethan and Joe skidded to a stop outside the open door of Mason's study. The "victim" wrapped her arms around my intended's neck, holding on as if hell's dominions were after her.

Mimi raised a tear-streaked face from Ethan's shoulder. "I took a break. When I came back, I found her. It had to have just happened. I thought it was part of the game at first. Someone to play the part of another victim, but it's not. It's not. She's really dead!"

The pretty girl wailed and hid her face in Ethan's shoulder. He appeared to struggle with an octopus as he tried to disentangle himself from her.

I peeked past Joe. Renee "Bella Donna" Richards lay sideways on the chaise. Scissors, buried to the handle, poked from the center of her chest. Dark eyes stared heavenward as we remained wedged in the doorway. Curtains billowed from open French-style doors. My gaze fell to the floor.

Muddy footprints cut a path across the mahogany floor.

Renee had to be the third or fourth dead body I'd seen in the last few months. Mae Belle's death had been difficult enough, and although cousins, we'd been virtually strangers.

Renee was my nemesis from as far back as high school. That made us almost sisters, didn't it? At the sight of her usually vibrant and vicious self lying lifeless, my heart grew heavy.

Joe bolted forward. Despite the telltale spread of blood across the upholstery, he felt for a pulse. "This isn't part of the game. You're right. She's dead. She hasn't been here but a few minutes. She's still warm." He whipped his cell phone from his pocket, punched in a number, and barked orders.

Snapping his phone closed, he turned to us.

"Ethan, get these people back. Keep them out of here. April, take care of Mimi. Summer, come here."

Wow, I felt privileged. I squared my shoulders, tilted my chin upward, and stepped forward. I stumbled slightly on the edge of the Oriental rug but quickly regained my composure and joined Joe.

"I know you were referring to the game when you said you'd solved the case, but can you elaborate?" Joe had moved to "Big Police Man" mode, furrowed brow, deepened lines around his mouth. He pulled a pen and small spiral notebook out of the back pocket of his pants.

My voice shook. "Renee, uh, Bella Donna, did it in the study with the poison. Belladonna to be exact. The suspect slipped it into the victim's drink." He had to be impressed.

"When was the last time you spoke with her?" I stood on my tiptoes to try and see what he wrote. He shifted the pad. "On the patio. With Ethan. I tried questioning her about Mae Belle's murder." I glanced again at the body.

"Then I saw her outside the bathroom with Mason. He had his arm around her. That was maybe ten or fifteen minutes ago. Do you think he did it?"

Joe's scowl deepened. Sirens wailed in the distance. "I can't discuss that with you. During your snooping, did you see anyone come in here with, or after, Renee?"

Could it be possible that Joe valued my insight—finally? "No, I was in the restroom with Ethan." At Joe's raised eyebrow look, I added, "Searching for the poison. Here." I handed him the pill bottle. "It's fake."

I glanced at Renee. "But I did see those scissors in the drawer." I shoved past him to double-check the desk. No scissors. "And those doors have been closed all night. Plus, I'm sure you've noticed the footprints."

"Yes, Sherlock, I have. And, as usual, you're contaminating a crime scene. Stop touching things."

"What's going on here?" Mason shoved through his guests. His gaze fell on Renee. He moaned and dropped to his knees beside her.

"Don't touch the body," Joe said as the other man reached out a hand.

"Oh Renee." Tears welled in Mason's eyes. Either he felt remorseful, was a good actor, or was innocent. "Who would do this?" He pushed to his feet. Sobs shook his shoulders, and he sagged against the nearest chair.

"Mr. White, I need to ask you to remain calm. Have a seat on the sofa. The other officers will be here any moment to ask you and your guests some questions. We need to make sure no one leaves. I'd also like a guest list."

Ethan seemed more than happy to relinquish crowd control to the arriving police. He stepped into the room and put an arm around my shoulders. "Are you all right?"

I nodded and nestled into him. A sudden chill ran up my spine.

Mason wouldn't have had time to commit the murder, run out the door, scale the patio wall, and arrive back in here. Even if he was a sprinter, he'd at least be breathing hard.

I pulled Ethan with me to the French doors. "Contrary to my first beliefs, I don't think Mason killed Mae Belle or Renee. He seems genuinely upset. Plus, he wouldn't do it during his own party, would he? That would be stupid. He's the first person the cops will suspect. Well, at least I would."

I stepped outside. The yard glowed beneath strung party lights. Except for this side.

I leaned over the railing. A string of unlit bulbs hung in a trail to the ground. Footprints sank in the mud of the flower beds and trailed off into a row of trees opposite the lawn. "Come on." I scaled the short patio wall and landed

with a dull thud.

Ethan made the drop with one bound. Hand in hand we raced for the trees, stopping just inside the tree line. "I cannot believe you've roped me into this again," he whispered. "My guess is Mason did it. He ran track in high school, I found out he was having an affair with Renee, and. . ."

"How did you find out? I suspected days ago. Do you think Mason might have an accomplice?"

He shrugged. "I took a cue from you and listened. Guys do listen sometimes."

"Maybe we'll get lucky and find someone else to add to the suspect list." I refused to believe I could be that far off on my suspicions. No one from my list besides Mason and Renee had attended the party.

That meant any one of them could have come here and killed her. And why had Ethan not filled me in on his new information? We'd be having a serious talk when we got home.

"Joe's going to have a fit that we left. Having you as my fiancée puts a damper on mine and Joe's friendship." Ethan winked.

"We'll be back before he knows. He won't disown you. April's your sister." I stopped and pulled my flashlight from a pocket of my dress. Ethan raised his eyebrows.

I shrugged. "Just in case I needed it."

"Uh-huh." He took it from me and scanned the trail in front of us. "Whoever we're following has shoe prints larger than yours and smaller than mine. Could be man or woman."

"See, Mason could never have made it out this far, and he's almost as tall as you."

"This doesn't mean anything. These footprints could be a day old. They could belong to the gardener."

Maybe, but I refused to admit it. Besides, I enjoyed running through the dark with Ethan by my side. We spent so little time alone, thanks to my two guard dogs, Aunt Eunice and Uncle Roy. I tugged on his hand. "Let's go just a little farther."

"You should go back."

I shook my head. "You can't leave me. I'm safer with you."

Something crashed through the brush. Ethan yanked me down. We hunkered behind a leafy bush. Ethan clicked off the flashlight, and I strained to see. Amazing how many sounds the woods had at night. Eerie. Mason didn't do a very good job of keeping the underbrush of his property cleared.

I swatted a low-hanging branch away from my

face and scooted closer to my protector. "Is it an animal?"

Ethan shrugged. "Maybe." He rose, pulling me with him. "Let's head back. If we're close to the person who killed Renee, we're putting ourselves in harm's way. We'll tell Joe about the cut string of lights and the footprints. Let him make his own conclusion."

I glanced over my shoulder. The moon cast enough light through the trees that I could make out the shape of a person hiding behind a juniper bush. "Ethan, there's someone there."

He whirled. "Hey, you!"

The figure darted away from us. We flicked the flashlight back on and pursued. A baseball cap and trench coat made it impossible to determine the gender. Our flight through the trees startled some bats, which flew over our heads. It would have been a contest to see who screeched louder. Them or me.

Where did Ethan get his stamina? My breath came in gasps. A pain stabbed my side. "Slow down, Ethan."

"We've almost caught him. I think there's a fence up ahead." He leaped over a log, dragging me with him. My hip smacked against the bark. Ethan slowed long enough to ask if I was all right then lurched ahead.

The person in front of us stopped, turned, and raised one arm. Ethan shoved me to the ground as a shot rang over our heads.

21

Ethan's breath stirred the air by my ear. "You aren't hit, are you?"

"No. I'm fi ne." If you didn't count the threat of my heart thumping out of my chest and the risk of being crushed by my fiancé.

Renee was killed by scissors; now we were being shot at. Could it be the same person or someone completely new?

He pulled me to a crouch. Keeping me behind him, Ethan stared in the direction of the mystery guest. He, or she, had vanished. Ethan took my hand and led me at a brisk walk back to Mason's house.

Joe met us halfway across the lawn, gun in hand. "I heard a shot."

Ethan placed an arm around my shoulders and pulled me close to stop my trembling. "We followed the footprints into the woods. We saw someone dressed in a baseball cap and trench coat, and we followed. The person shot at us."

"No one hurt?" Joe's gaze skimmed over us.

"We're fine, but I'd like to get Summer inside."

Joe barked orders and motioned for a couple of officers to head in the direction we'd come. "You never should have pursued a suspect. You could have been killed. Besides possibly contaminating evidence by scaling the patio wall."

He shook his head. "I expect this type of behavior from Summer, but I credited you with more sense, Ethan."

"Got caught up in the moment. When we did see someone, it seemed natural to follow." He steered me past my cousin, into the living room, and deposited me on a sofa next to April.

A pretty girl in a maid uniform offered me a glass of wine. I shook my head. "Water would be wonderful, though." She scurried off to fetch my drink.

April pulled a cashmere throw from behind me and placed it around my shoulders.

Tremors subsiding, I grinned. Despite another near brush with death, the thrill of pursuit coursed through me. Call me mental, but I'd developed a fondness for the rush of the chase. The closeness of solving a mystery. The danger. The drawback being that I often involved someone I cared about.

"I can't believe you're smiling." April folded her arms. "I thank God you didn't drag me into those dark woods. That farmer's house was terrifying enough. Now you've got my brother hooked. Yes"—she nodded at my stunned look—

"that's exactly what it is. You're addicted."

"Ethan is a grown man. I'm not forcing him to help me."

"Yes, you are. He loves you. He's going to do

whatever it takes to keep you safe. Even if it means going with you on your wild-goose chases. Had it even entered your silly head that he could have been shot out there? He's my brother!" She stood and glowered at me.

"No! None of the victims have been shot. How was I supposed to know? But I made a promise. . ."

"Oh please. Don't try to justify yourself. Last time, you wanted to save a woman who reminded you of the night your parents died. Now, it's a promise to someone you didn't care much for in the first place."

My mouth dropped open. I'd never seen April this angry. "I don't know what to say."

"Say you'll stop. Before something bad happens." She stomped her foot.

"I can't. I received threatening letters."

"Again—you're justifying. Why don't you just take the hint?" She spun and marched from the room, brushing past the maid with my water.

I accepted the offered glass and stared into its depths. My friend was right. I'd use any means to justify solving this mystery. I couldn't fault her feelings. She only cared about her brother. Maybe I should leave things to Joe and his fellow officers. But could I? And Ethan. What did I do about him?

Should I break off our engagement until the case was solved? If he wasn't around me, he'd be safe. Tears welled. Would he even take me back if I did that? I set the water on the coffee table.

"What's on your mind?" I raised my head to see Ethan leaning against the doorjamb. His hair was mussed from our run. Most of the powder had disappeared, turning him back into the handsome thirty-three-year-old I fell in love with.

"You and April have a fight?" I shrugged, blinking and swallowing against what promised to be a doozy of a sob fest. Ethan sat next to me and took my hands in his. "Talk to me."

"I can't keep doing this to you." I sniffed. "April's right. I'm addicted. I need to go to a recovery group or something. I need to break up with you until I'm healed."

"What?" He chuckled then straightened. His smile faded. "You're serious?"

"I can't keep putting you in danger. It isn't fair." Squaring my shoulders, I took a deep breath and forced myself to stare into his eyes. "I'm calling off the wedding until I find Mae Belle's killer. Then if you still want me, and I've recovered from my crazy obsession, we'll resume our relationship."

"What did my sister say to you?" The pained look on Ethan's face almost undid my steely resolve.

"She told me the truth." I stood, letting the throw fall to the cushions. I pulled Ethan's ring from my finger and placed it on the coffee table. "I can't put you in harm's way. Don't worry about me." My chin quivered. "I'll get a ride home."

"Summer." His voice broke.

Forcing my back to remain straight, my gaze focused on the door, I marched from the room, down the hall, and out the front door. It wasn't until a mile down the road that the tears I'd been holding spilled down my cheeks.

I wrapped my arms around myself to ward off

the gut-wrenching pain. The hurt I'd just caused Ethan was nothing compared to what I'd experience should something happen to him because of my stubbornness to continue this detective thing.

Lights cut through the night as an automobile crested the top of a hill. I darted behind a bush as Ethan's truck sped in the direction of my house. I settled in, making a seat in a pile of pine needles until I deemed enough time had passed and he'd given up and gone home.

My finger felt naked without the weight of his ring. I rubbed the empty spot, and the flow of tears increased. I was a doofus. I was willing to forgo something wonderful, for something that might get me killed. Why did Ethan waste his time on me?

At the thought, a sob escaped until the woods resonated with the sound of my cries. I wrapped my arms around my bent knees and gave in to the grief. If the trench coat–covered suspect heard me, I wouldn't put up a fight. Gun or not.

A twig snapped. I leaped to my feet. Maybe I was a coward after all and still in love with life. Fleeing seemed the best option.

A branch slapped my face. I put a hand to my cheek and felt wetness that didn't come from tears. Icy tentacles of fear spurred me away from an unseen predator. Having been lost in the ache of my rash decision, I hadn't headed back to the road.

Instead, I found myself in unfamiliar territory, fighting to remove my tangled hair from a tree's spiky fingers. When had I lost the wig? During my flight from Ethan? The sweater I wore did little to ward off the evening chill.

Silence echoed around me. I stopped in a clearing and stared into the night sky. I should have paid more attention to Ethan's explanations of the stars. I had no idea which way to turn.

Snap!

I whirled and ran, putting a hand to my chest to keep my heart from pounding free of my rib cage.

Lord, help me. What had I done? Leaving Ethan dejected on the sofa of Mason's home then running blind. Whispers scratched through the woods, following me in my panic. I'd been calmer a few months ago, running through the woods with a madman singing my name. A silent pursuer sent jolts of terror through me. I much preferred knowing who stalked me. And, again, I'd left my cell phone at home. Idiot!

"Hello?" A woman's voice. I turned from side to side and tried to determine the direction. "Helloooo!"

I opened my mouth to answer then clamped it shut. If she was the one seeking me, I wouldn't volunteer my position. Let her search. I hunkered behind some thick brush to wait.

Clouds moved, obscuring the moon and casting me into darkness so thick I thought I could move it aside with my hand. Instead of frightening me further, it soothed me. If I couldn't see her, she couldn't find me, right? I breathed as slowly and quietly as possible, measuring each breath with an invisible ruler. Timing each rise and fall of my chest.

My eyes adjusted, and I could make out shadows. No more eerie greetings floated through the night. I pushed the illumination button on my watch. Ten o'clock. The green glow shone like a searchlight.

Horror. I clapped a hand over the face to hide it and shook my head at my stupidity.

Leaves rustled overhead, disturbed by unseen animals. I felt myself becoming one with my surroundings and envisioned myself as queen of the forest. Queen of the foolish was more like it. How long until the woman of the ghostly voice stepped into the clearing?

How much time had passed? Five minutes? Ten? *Lord, why didn't You give me patience?* I took the question back as soon as I asked. Patience really wasn't something I wanted Him to teach me. I'd seen what others had gone through after asking. Maybe I'd ask for wisdom. Another thing I seemed to be lacking.

footfall sounded nearby. I held my breath. What *was* the woman doing? My body tensed in expectation of pouncing when she came in my sight. Armed with nothing but my flashlight. . .I patted my pockets. Nope. Ethan still had it. My only weapon would be the element of surprise.

There! I launched, tackling her. The air left her in a *whoosh.*

The clouds parted. I stared into a familiar face

22

Sherry, Mae Belle's former secretary, rolled me to the forest floor. I spun and landed on my face, spitting out dirt and dried leaves, then leaped to my feet quicker than the chubby woman across from me.

"Why are you chasing me?"

"I have no idea what you're talking about." She stood and brushed mud from the seat of her pants. Her expression remained bland, as her gaze shifted over my left shoulder.

"Then what are you doing out here?"

"Looking for bats." Her gaze ran over me. "What are you doing out here, dressed in. . .What *are* you wearing?"

"A costume." A draft blew across my backside. I glanced behind me, moving like a dog chasing its tail, until I caught a glimpse of my behind. A large rip in the back separated the bodice partly from the skirt of the dress, exposing my polka-dot

undies. Thinking myself clever, I'd purposely matched them to the dress. Thankfully, the woods were dark. If only

I could ward off the night breeze. And keep my back from Sherry's sight.

"Oh, that's right. You're one of the privileged few to attend Mason White's party while the rest of us stomp through the woods in search of more *innocent* pleasure. Everyone knows what kinds of things go on at his parties. Then they judge everyone else, instead of looking at their own exploits."

She rummaged through a pile of dead brush and pulled out a striped canvas duffel bag. "If you don't mind, I'll be on my way. Have a good evening."

"What's in the bag, Sherry? A hat, a coat, a gun?" Maybe it was my imagination, but the woman seemed awfully defensive about Mason's party.

"You're insane." She held the bag behind her back. "It's just bat-hunting tools."

"Why are you hiding it?" I lunged for the bag. Sherry stepped backward, tripped over a log, and landed on a briar bush. If I hadn't thought I was staring at the one who shot at me, I would've laughed.

A crash through the brush sent Sherry scrambling for cover, dragging her bag of tricks behind her. I dove into a thicket. Peeking from my hiding place, I couldn't locate Sherry. For a large woman, she moved silently.

On my hands and knees, I scurried in the direction I thought the road would be and prayed the movement through the woods belonged to an animal. A small one with no teeth or claws.

My knees caught in what was left of my skirt

and ripped the fabric further. With one hand, I bunched the clothes around my waist and duck-walked the rest of the way, keeping my head low.

A horn honked. I hadn't ventured as far into the woods as I'd thought. Straightening, I darted in the direction of the sound and what promised freedom from shadows and weird night time rodent hunters.

I burst from the bushes, narrowly missing becoming road kill as a truck sped past. The piece of dress I'd held in order not to flash my unmentionables ripped from my hand and whipped like a tattered flag to snag on a bush.

Wonderful. Before another car could pass and catch me in a state of disarray, I tied my sweater sarong-style around my waist. It didn't cover everything, leaving most of my right thigh bare, but hopefully it was enough to keep me from being arrested for indecent exposure.

Goose pimples rising on the flesh of my arms, I began my trek home. After a mile, the cheap pumps I'd slipped on my feet rubbed blisters the size of molehills on my heels. I kicked them off, leaving them on the side of the road. Several times I found myself close to tears as another fit of shivering overtook me.

Loneliness formed a heavy cloud over me, so thick I thought I'd suffocate. The absence of vehicles traveling in either direction clarified the stupidity of running through the night. At this point I wasn't picky. I'd go anywhere something with four wheels headed. Somewhere there would be people.

I brushed aside Uncle Roy's warnings of

hitchhiking. Being alone left me with too much time to think, and I remembered how I'd ended in that predicament. Best friend or not, April could jump in a lake. I'd get my ring back from Ethan, if he'd accept my apology, and let God handle our safety. I was a fool to think otherwise.

To take my mind off my aching feet and chilly bottom, I mulled over the facts from Mae Belle's death. Two victims, both stabbed. Two different weapons. One bloody glove in a Dumpster. I made a mental note to ask Joe whether he'd found out who it belonged to. A threatening letter.

A chocolate-covered rat. A kitten. Oh yeah. They didn't count. Stupid game.

Someone taking shots at me and Ethan. I shook my head. Nothing tied together. The whole thing wound tighter than a proficient liar's alibi.

Sherry burst from a stand of evergreens ahead of me, not looking in my direction, and marched forward. How had she gotten in front of me? Did she live close by? She seemed to know these woods well.

My thoughts scattered. I quickened my pace to keep her in sight, still wondering what the canvas bag slung over her shoulder contained. My stocking feet were rasped by the decaying foliage on the road's shoulder.

A car sat on the crest of the hill. Sherry increased her pace, approached the sedan, tossed the bag through an open window, slid behind the wheel, then sped away. Wonderful.

I crossed my arms tighter around myself, hunched my shoulders, and continued the next mile home.

Clouds obscured the moon. I stared at the ground to gauge where to place my next step. Small sticks and stones poked my feet. How long until my family realized I hadn't

made it home?

Lights pierced the darkness. I paused by the roadside, my left thumb extended in the universal language of hitchhikers. At this point, I no longer cared how I looked or how I'd get home.

The vehicle swerved toward me, not slowing. I squinted, trying to make out the driver before I flung myself behind a stout tree. I felt the *whoosh* as the car sped past.

Moments later, tires squealed as the driver turned for another pass. I tore myself out of the prickly bush I'd landed in and plunged headlong back into the woods.

I couldn't tell whether the car trying to run me over was the same one Sherry had climbed into. A four-door sedan; I knew that much. I pressed the button on my watch. Eleven o'clock. Had it really only been an hour since I'd left Mason's?

Time dragged as slow as Uncle Roy when the leaves needed raking in the fall. I should be close enough to home to keep a straight path parallel and come out in my front yard. *Please, Lord, let it be so.*

After the longest mile of my life, I shoved my way past low-hanging branches to the freedom of my lawn. A light greeted me. The glow from the kitchen window was the most beautiful sight I'd seen in what seemed like eons. I dashed across the cool grass and up the stairs to the porch.

"Summer?" Ethan rose from one of the rocking chairs. "What happened? Your clothes—"

"Ethan!" I threw myself in his arms. "I'm sorry. Forget everything I said. I love you. Can I have your ring back?"

"*What* happened?" He held me at arm's length.

"I ripped my dress fighting my way through the woods between here and Mason's. Then I tackled Sherry because it really seemed like she was following me, although she said she was searching for bats. Likely story. She had a bag. I never did find out what was in it. Then I had to leave my shoes.

"Oh, and I tied the sweater around my waist, because, well, you can see." I gestured at my waist. My words rose and fell with the rapidity of my breathing. "Then I tried to hitchhike—dangerous, I know—and someone tried to run me over. Oh Ethan. All I could think about was what a fool I was and getting home to you. Why didn't you come get me?" If he could make anything out of my rambling, I hoped it was that I was sorry.

He ran a hand through his hair. "I tried. I drove up and down the highway at least five times. There was no sign of you. I came here to wait. Frantic something might have happened to you." He swiped his thumb across my cheek. "You're bleeding."

"A branch tried slapping some sense into me." I cupped my palms around his face. "I'm sorry. I really am."

Ethan smiled. "As delightful as you look, you really need to get in the house and get some clothes on."

"May I please have the ring back?" Tears stung the backs of my eyes. "Will you forgive me?"

"There's nothing to forgive. I've already spoken to April. She feels awful. Said she said those things out of fear and can't imagine not having you for a sister." Ethan dug into the pocket of his pants. Taking my left hand in his, he slid the ring back onto my finger. "I love you, Summer. Crazy, emotional, and spontaneous as you might be." He brushed the hair back from my face. "Let's get you dressed and call Joe. Let him try and make sense of your story."

The gravel on the driveway crunched. A car idled near the road, its windows as dark and vacant as a phantom's face.

Ethan took several steps toward it, and the dark-colored sedan roared away.

178

23

For the third time in less than six months, I found myself in a tight spot. Graduating from receiving threatening letters to being shot at and being spied on, I was intelligent enough to know what came next. A face-to-face encounter that resulted in sharp wits to stay alive. And to put icing on the cake, so to speak, I'd been presented with the deed to Mae Belle's business. Why'd the silly woman leave it to me?

Was the rift between her and Aunt Claudia that wide, that deep? And did Aunt Claudia know, having left without the deed?

I shivered and slid the dark chocolate-covered candy from the dipping belt. Laying it on the tray, I swirled an *S* on top with my finger.

Thankfully, Ethan had forgiven my idiotic attempts to save him from me. April apologized profusely for taking her fear of losing Ethan out on me. Joe knew nothing. No leads on the glove, the letter, or the twice-murdering suspect. If he did know anything, he wasn't sharing the information with me. More reason for me to keep my promise to Mae Belle.

I shrugged, not willing to give up, no matter the danger to myself. Same as the last two mysteries I'd gotten involved in. I suspected, but never knew for sure, who the bad guys were until they held a gun to my head. Literally.

This time, the clues hid so deep I wasn't sure I'd be able to sort them out. The facts had to be right in front of me. I just needed to be able to see them.

I stared at a nearby assortment of chocolate. What did I have to bite into to discover the creamy center of this case? Why couldn't life be like an assortment of fine chocolate?

"Summer! Wake up." Eunice plopped another tray in front of me.

I jerked at her outburst. "You about scared me out of my wits, Aunt Eunice."

"I'm taking off early today. Don't forget we're meeting the men for dinner at that new restaurant." With those words, she grabbed her purse and dashed out the door.

Five trays of undipped creams taunted me from the table. There was no way I'd have time to dip the candy, go home to change, then meet Ethan and my aunt and uncle. I glanced down at my jeans and long-sleeved T-shirt.

At least the restaurant wasn't very dressy. Most pizza places weren't, and I didn't think any outfit I picked could compete with the half-undressed look I'd sported a couple of nights before.

Time passed with the repetition of dipping creams. A glance at my watch told me I was an hour late. My shoulder ached from bending over the dipping machine for two hours then sorting the candy into their respective cases. I quickly rubbed my shoulder before grabbing my purse and locking the candy store.

I turned and marched to the spinning neon sign advertising the best pizza in town. Scents of warm yeast and tomato sauce greeted me as I barged through the front door, almost knocking down Larry Bell in my haste.

"Excuse me." I placed a hand on his shoulder to steady myself.

He jerked away and darted through the door. Hubert and Edna sat cozily in a corner booth. Lewis Anderson leaned against the counter and appeared to be studying a menu mounted on the wall. Except for Mason and Sherry, it seemed my entire suspect list had a craving for pizza at the new pizzeria's grand opening. This was the perfect opportunity to observe them and remain undetected.

A grinning teenage girl with a swinging ponytail directed me to the banquet room. I pushed through the saloon-style doors.

"Surprise!"

"Happy birthday!"

Friends and family shouted and tossed iridescent-colored confetti in my direction. Ethan grabbed me, dipped me over his arm, and kissed me before saying, "Happy thirtieth, Tink."

My head spun when he righted me. I couldn't believe I'd been so wrapped up in the case that I'd forgotten my own birthday. April slapped a party hat on my head and snapped the elastic under my chin. "Ow!"

"Stop being a baby." She gave me a big hug. "Bet you thought everyone forgot, didn't you?"

"Actually I forgot." My cheeks hurt from smiling.

"Right. You never pass up an opportunity to be the center of attention."

Aunt Eunice wrapped her arms around me. "I'm sorry I dashed off and left you with all that work." She grinned. "But I had a good reason."

I placed a kiss on her cheek. "You are the best, Aunt Eunice."

"I know." She kissed me back. "Let's eat, then we'll have cake and presents."

After the stress of circumstances since Mae Belle's death, the camaraderie with my family and friends gave me a grin that hurt my cheeks. My mood lightened. The pile of gifts brought tears to my eyes.

Aunt Eunice thrust a package into my hands. "Open mine first. It's a computer program that will enable you to keep track of all your leads."

I smiled at her. "Glad you could keep it a surprise."

Ethan's gift was the niftiest little handheld camera with a powerful zoom lens. They'd all given me something to do with solving mysteries. Joe, bless his cop-thinking heart, said he'd had the phone company put a GPS tracker on my new cell phone.

Tears coursed down my cheeks. "I thought y'all wanted me to stop?"

"Sweetheart." Ethan cupped my face and wiped

my tears away with his thumbs. "This is who you are. This nosiness, this craziness, this unshakable need to help others, despite your insisting God didn't give you compassion." He grinned. "None of us want you to change. We love you just the way you are. Happy birthday."

I wanted to marry the man that instant. Why wait until spring? Never mind that I didn't have a dress, a cake, or a caterer.

Ethan steered me to a seat and plopped a plastic tiara on my head. April placed a plate of pizza and a glass of soda in front of me.

"Y'all are spoiling me." Tears stung my eyes. "This is the happiest day of my life."

"Not for long." Aunt Eunice nodded toward the glass door.

Sherry barged through, slamming the swinging door panels against the wall. She glared at the group before zeroing in on me. She reminded me of a picture I'd seen of an enraged bull. And I was the waving red cape. "You had this planned the entire time!"

"Excuse me?" I had the urge to hide behind Ethan's broad shoulders.

"A Dream Wedding." She stepped into my personal space. I drew back to keep our noses from touching. "I found this." She waved a sheet of pink stationery in front of my face. "Mae Belle said she'd make me her partner!"

I took the paper from her. Mae Belle apparently kept a handwritten will at her former place of business in addition to a copy at her lawyer's office. I handed the sheet back to Sherry.

"You can buy the business from me. I don't want it."

Her eyes almost bugged out of her head. "Where am I supposed to get that kind of money?"

Aunt Eunice grabbed my arm and dragged me to a corner of the room. "Are you as crazy as Sherry? She's on your suspect list. Has it occurred to you that she might have killed Mae Belle to get the store? Now you own it, and you're willing to hand it to her? She might try to kill you off as well."

The thought had occurred to me. Especially after meeting her in the woods. "With Sherry managing A Dream Wedding, she'll be where I can keep an eye on her. Plus, if it is the store she wants, she won't have to kill anymore to get it. I'll have time to prove her guilty or not. I really don't want the silly thing."

"Fine." Aunt Eunice released me and folded her arms. "Just don't come crying to me when you wind up dead."

"I won't." I turned back to Sherry. "One question, Sherry. How did you get that letter?"

Her face reddened. "Uh, I uh. . ."

"You stole it. You've been snooping around, and I'm willing to bet you weren't searching for bats in the woods. I'm guessing that canvas bag you dragged around had things from the store in it. Am I correct?" I raised my eyebrows.

"Yes." She narrowed her eyes. "But it's my stuff. Things owed to me. I knew once you cleaned the place out, it'd be too late."

"Why did you park outside my house the other night?

After your supposed bat hunt?" Okay, it was two questions, but she seemed willing to communicate. Kind of. "You're crazy, do you know that? I have no idea what you're talking about."

I gnawed my lower lip and stared at the woman in front of me. Could I trust her to run the place? It's not like there were any customers. If she wanted Mae Belle dead, she'd have waited until she owned the business.

"Fine. I'll be making an inventory tomorrow, and I'll know whether you took anything else. You can work there until you either buy it from me, or I decide what to do with it." I folded my arms and glared until she turned and barged out the door.

"I sure hope you're doing the right thing." Aunt Eunice stood beside me.

"You and me both." I watched through the large window of the banquet room as Sherry marched to her dark-colored sedan. She glanced to her left before climbing behind the wheel. I stepped closer to the glass and squinted.

Mason and Larry Bell were throwing punches at each other under the parking lot lights.

24

Joe and Ethan dashed past me. Aunt Eunice and I tried crowding through the door at the same time. My hip banged against the door frame. She grunted when we got stuck, and I stepped back to let her pass. By the time we'd reached the parking lot, Joe and Ethan held the fighters apart.

Mason and Larry now hurled words instead of fists.

"How dare you judge me!" Mason spat his words at Larry while trying to pull free of Ethan's grip on his arm. "Let go."

"Every man shall be judged." Larry stood complacent with Joe's hands clamped on his shoulders. "You are a whoremonger."

"I won't be criticized by the likes of you. Let go, Banning." He jerked loose and swung a punch at Ethan's face, connecting with the sound of someone slapping a side of beef.

Ethan's lip split, splattering his shirt with drops of blood. "Hey! Your problem isn't with me."

He wrapped Mason in a bear hug. Mason drew back his head then thrust it forward into Ethan's nose. Ethan released his grip and stumbled backward. My poor baby was getting mangled.

I leaped into the fray, launching onto Mason's back like an infant orangutan on its mother. Not to be outdone, Aunt Eunice slapped Larry across the cheek.

"What's that for? I'm just standing here!"

"Eunice, that's assault." Joe released Larry and grasped Eunice's hand.

"Looked to me like he wanted to get in there and hit someone, so I stopped him." She pulled free of Joe, planted her fists on her hips, and transferred her attention to me.

"Need any help, Summer? This one's subdued."

"No, I got it." I tightened my hold around Mason's neck. He spun like a top to try and dislodge me.

Uncle Roy marched across the parking lot with his trusty rifle and aimed for the sky. I'd told him a million times that only rednecks drove around with a gun rack in their truck. Would the man ever listen to me?

"You shoot that gun, Roy, and I'm arresting you." Joe grabbed for the weapon. "Why you keep it stashed in your truck is beyond me."

Uncle Roy clutched it to his chest and darted back to his Chevy.

"Grab him, Ethan!" Larry swung wildly at Mason, barely missing my head.

"Get her off me, Banning!" Mason turned to brush me off by slamming into the nearest car. The breath left me in a *whoosh,* and pain radiated through my lower back.

Ethan wrapped his arms around my waist and

yanked. "Thanks for the help, sweetheart, but I can handle this." He set me on my feet and threw a punch that knocked Mason to the asphalt. Mason stared at us from the ground, his right eye reddening.

"Had enough?" Ethan offered a hand to help the man to his feet.

Mason nodded and grasped it. "My beef wasn't with you. It's with that know-it-all little twerp Bell."

"You still can't brawl in a public place." Joe scowled, one hand clutching Larry, the other regaining its grip on Aunt Eunice.

"Then arrest me." Mason rubbed his knuckles.

"Why don't you tell me what started this." Joe released his captives and withdrew a pad of paper and pencil from his pocket.

"This man is swine." Larry tilted his chin toward Mason.

"An adulterer."

"I'm not married, and neither was Renee. You're probably the one who killed her. You and your self-righteous ways."

"Immorality runs rampant in Mountain Shadows."

"And you've elected yourself as cleanup crew?"

My neck swiveled like a lawn sprinkler between the two men. This was the best birthday entertainment ever.

Aunt Eunice sported a grin that rivaled the Cheshire cat. April had joined us at some point and sat perched on the hood of my car. She clutched a handful of tissues.

My elation dropped a notch when I noticed the blood dripping from Ethan's nose. He'd tried unsuccessfully to stanch the flow with a festively decorated napkin.

"Oh." I rushed to his side. "I'm so sorry. Let me help you. Is it broken?"

He shook his head. "Happy birthday, Summer."

"It is. Very entertaining."

He frowned.

"Except for your battered face."

"Uh-huh." Ethan raised his head toward the sky. "Go put your pretty little nose where it wants to be."

Mason took a step toward Larry. Joe stiff-armed him to keep him away from the other man. "Look, Mason. Either you stop the aggression, or I'm hauling you to the station."

"Haul *him* in, the little weasel."

Larry kept an impassive expression on his bland face. " must go about the Lord's work, Mr. White. And fornication is an abomination." His voice rose until he almost shouted.

Who would have thought Larry to be a self-proclaimed prophet? I exchanged glances with April. She shrugged. We needed to search deeper into Larry's involvement with Mae Belle. If the man had been planning a wedding, where was the bride? If he'd wanted a party, where were the friends? And what was up with Mason's defensive attitude?

My head ached from all the questions. My back throbbed.

I sidled next to April. "So, who do you think we

should check out? Mason and his blatant disregard for moral values, or the up-and-coming evangelist?"

"Who's on your list?"

"Sherry, but I've got her covered. Anderson, the funeral director, Mason, Hubert Smith, Edna Mobley, and Larry Bell. We can rule out Renee, for obvious reasons." I sighed. Not liking her didn't remove my sadness at the way she'd died.

"Speaking of suspects." I motioned to the other side of the lot. Hubert ushered Edna from the pizza parlor and gave our group a wide berth. Edna caught me looking and ducked her head.

Larry stepped in their direction and pointed. "More infidels!"

Joe snapped his notebook closed. "That's enough, Larry. If I didn't know better, I'd think you'd been drinking." He leaned closer and sniffed. "You don't smell like you have. Go home, and leave others alone."

"Remember the plank in your own eye before you go pointing out the splinters in other people's." Aunt Eunice nodded to emphasize her point.

A plank in Larry's eye? Did she know something about the man?

I'd neglected my suffering fiancé long enough. I made a mental note to get with my aunt later tonight.

I joined Ethan as he leaned against his truck. "Are you ready to go? We should probably put some ice on your nose."

"I thought maybe you forgot about me." He smiled and winked. "Ow."

"Let me get Uncle Roy to carry my gifts, and

I'll meet you back here."

The bleeding had stopped by the time we reached my house, but I led Ethan inside, situated him on a kitchen chair, then made a pack for his nose out of a washcloth and plastic bag full of ice.

Uncle Roy deposited my gifts on the kitchen table, and Aunt Eunice prepared a pot of coffee.

"Whooee! What a party." She leaned against the counter.

Joe strolled in behind April and plopped into a chair next to Ethan. "A parking lot brawl is not a celebration."

"What's the plank in Larry's eye?" I stared at my aunt and rubbed Ethan's temples.

"No gossip." Joe reached for a mug and held it out for Aunt Eunice to fill.

"It's common knowledge that Larry found himself an Internet girlfriend. He spouted the news all over town. Then Mae Belle, bless her heart, decided to try it for herself. Must have been before she got involved with that funeral director. Or maybe he's what she found on the cyber highway of love."

Aunt Eunice poured a drink for Uncle Roy. "Anyway, turned out it was all a scam. Larry's been bitter ever since. Said Mae Belle ran his love away. Took it upon himself to be the conscience of Mountain Shadows. He's been upsetting a lot of people. Mason ain't the only one who's mad at the guy."

"It's sad that Larry got scammed, but it doesn't give him the right to go poking his nose into everyone's business." Which reminded me to check on Ethan. The bleeding hadn't resumed.

"Look who's talking." Joe clunked his mug on the table. "The Queen of Nosiness."

"I'm trying to solve a crime."

"For the hundredth time, it's not your job."

I took the stained washcloth from Ethan's swollen nose and rinsed it in the sink. Seemed like I had two mysteries to solve: Mae Belle's murder and the computer scam involving Larry.

Maybe his mystery "love" had something to do with my cousin's death. If Mae Belle put a stop to a scam earning a lot of money, that would be reason enough to shut her up, wouldn't it?

Aunt Eunice set the coffeepot back on the stove. "And if that ain't bad enough, the man still harbors sore feelings over the fact that my friends Ruby and Mabel both turned him down when he asked them out. I think that was before he turned to the Internet. The poor fool hounded them for

weeks."

I leaned against the counter. "Who do you think killed Mae Belle and Renee, Joe?"

Joe choked on his coffee. "Why do you ask me questions you know I can't answer?"

"Not even off the record?" Fine. I'd tell him my own opinion. "Here's what I'm thinking."

Ethan crossed his arms and leaned back in his chair, April rolled her eyes, and Joe's shoulders slumped.

"Lots of people had a reason to do away with Mae Belle. She may be my cousin, but let's face it, the woman had an abrasive attitude. I still don't know why she went into a business working with people." I paced.

"Hubert Smith and Edna Mobley are upset because she ruined the plans for their wedding. Mason, who I don't really think is the murderer, tried using her to plan a party. He ended up planning one himself. But"—I paused and held up a hand—"what if Mae Belle found out about him and Renee?"

Joe opened his mouth to say something. I held up a hand to stop him.

"Then there's Lewis Anderson, who I've discovered was having an affair with Mae Belle. He could have killed her in order to hide his dirty secret from his wife. Then there's Larry Bell."

"Okay, Sherlock, who do you think did it?" Joe tilted his chin. "Who's at the top of your list?"

"I prefer Nancy Drew. I've told you that. Sherlock is a man. They're all pretty even on my suspect list. Renee was on there, but, well. . ." I plopped into a chair. "Maybe I do cause death and destruction everywhere I go. When the diamonds showed up under my rosebush, Terri Lee died. Then I found that girl at the carnival, now Mae Belle and Renee." A sob rose in my throat. "I just want to help people."

My shoulders slumped, and I bowed my head to stare at the floor. A spider scuttled across my line of vision. If I hadn't been so dejected, I would've jumped up and screamed.

Ethan rose and pulled me into his arms. "We know that, honey. None of this is your fault."

I stiffened and buried my face in his shirt. "Joe's always yelling at me; now April did."

"I said I was sorry," April said.

"I haven't yelled at you lately," Joe added, leaning back in his chair. "And I won't unless you break the law. You've got a good list of suspects compiled. I've been checking them, and they all have valid reasons for disliking Mae Belle. But none

of them seem like the killing sort. Just because you don't like someone doesn't mean you want them dead." He let the chair legs slam back to the floor.

"Forget it. I'm just feeling sorry for myself. I honestly thought I'd have this solved by now." I plopped into the nearest chair.

"We're focusing on the computer scam," Joe said. "There's your tidbit of free knowledge."

"The love interest's name is Lola." I turned, and the words burst from my mouth before I could hold them back.

Joe speared me with his gaze. "How do you know that?"

"Uh." I glanced at April. I might as well tell the truth. Joe would be less mad. "We went to visit Larry and got on his computer."

If Joe's crimson face was any indication, he'd be shouting at me very soon.

25

Sunday after church, I stood in front of A Dream Wedding and stared through the plate glass window as Sherry swept a broom briskly across the floor. A smile split her face.

Her back seemed straighter. And although I couldn't hear from outside, I'd guess she hummed as she worked.

Heavy clouds swirled overhead. I shook my head. This was the type of stormy weather we'd get in the spring, not in September. Not the norm, but not unheard of either.

A fat raindrop plopped on my head, and I turned, hitched my tote bag securely on my shoulder, and strolled toward Grandma's Story Corner. A venti-sized frozen coffee would brighten my day.

The cold drink numbed my hand. I meandered for the inspirational fiction aisle of the store. I'd long since given up on buying and reading detective how-to books. No matter how much information I gleaned from between the pages, I still did things my way. Which most of the time seemed haphazard. At least to anyone looking on.

I hoped there was some semblance of order to my madness. Despite all my mishaps, the bad guy did get it in the end.

I grabbed a book that showed promise, handed over the required cash, then took a seat at a round table in the coffee bar area. I tried to relax and submerge myself into the delightful love story printed for me to enjoy.

No use. My thoughts spun like the rising wind outside. I closed the book and grabbed my case notes from the tote bag I'd set on the floor.

Sunday afternoons were normally spent with Ethan, my aunt and uncle, or lazing around the house. With the speed my mind raced, I'd thought getting away would benefit me more. The details of the mystery haunted me, dogged my steps, and fogged my mind.

Thunder rumbled outside, and I glanced out the window. Rain fell in a steady curtain. I still smarted from the verbal deluge from Joe last night. It wasn't like April and I broke into Larry Bell's house or anything. The door had been unlocked.

Concentration still eluded me with each stroke of lightning across the slate gray sky. All my suspects had reason to dislike Mac Belle, but to murder her? I shook my head. Something teased at the corner of my mind. A clue I couldn't quite grasp.

What was it? I squeezed my plastic cup too hard. Coffee and whipped cream squirted from the hole in the top of the lid. Wonderful. I grabbed a napkin and wiped at my notes.

The pencil marks smeared in gray and brown smudges. Sitting here accomplished nothing. I gathered my soggy papers, tossed my half-empty cup in the garbage, then left the store. The rain had stopped, leaving the air heavy and still.

I set off at a brisk pace toward A Dream Wedding where I'd left my car. From the eerie green tinge to the sky, I didn't want to be out in the open much longer. By the time I reached my car, the wind whipped at my clothes and hair.

Debris hurtled across the street. I slid behind the wheel and inserted my key. A metal sign flipped through the air and bounced off the hood of my car. I screamed and ducked.

The air roared. I spotted the twister on its path of destruction, yanked open my car door, and leaped out. I needed to get under cover.

Traversing the sidewalk was like running a gauntlet of wood, paper, and anything else light enough to be picked up and thrown. Within minutes I'd be dodging items larger than a sign. I eyed the nearby cars.

I pulled at the door of A Dream Wedding. Locked. Where was my key? I fumbled through my purse with one hand and banged on the store window with the other.

The wind increased, along with my fear. I plastered myself against the glass and peered inside.

Sherry huddled in a corner of the store, eyes wide in a pale face.

"Let me in!"

She shook her head.

"Twister!" I pointed to my left.

She folded her arms around her knees and hid her face.

Crazy woman! I whipped my head around, looking for anywhere safer than where I stood. The air was so loud I could barely think.

I glanced back at Sherry. "Get away from the window!"

I sprinted down the street and around the corner to the nearest alley. There. Stairs leading to the basement opening of a business. A Dumpster partially covered the entrance. I

leaped the last few steps and crouched with my arms wrapped around the handrail as the world blew apart around me.

I closed my eyes against the stinging dirt and prayed. For everything. Forgiveness, wisdom, patience. Anything I could think of over the tornado's mighty roar.

Were Aunt Eunice and Uncle Roy in the storm shelter? What about Ethan and April? I even wondered about abrasive Sherry. Had she sought shelter or stayed huddled in the corner behind a huge plate glass window?

A shrill shriek caused my eyes to pop open. The Dumpster pulled away then rolled at high speed toward me. I screamed.

The small entrance I cowered in was too small for the steel devil. The square box hit the brick wall then bounced off. I hugged the steel handrail next to me.

I promised the Lord anything and everything as the world went crazy and stole my breath. My heart beat so high in my throat that I choked. I thought I might've cried, but the wind dried my eyes before the tears could escape.

My skin stung as if ants marched a biting trail over me, and my curls tangled around my head when the storm rolled away. I thanked the Lord I still breathed and rose shakily to my feet. Miraculously my purse still hung from my shoulder.

I bled from a few cuts on my arms but was otherwise unharmed. I stepped out of the alley and into mayhem.

My car stuck out through the window of A Dream Wedding. Other vehicles huddled against buildings like mourning spectators. Stunned people scuttled down uneven sidewalks. Some cried out names. I turned to face the other direction.

At the other end of the street, other than a shattered window, Summer Confections seemed to have survived. Another blessing from God. I continued my slow shuffle toward my wrecked Sonata.

Ethan stood in front of the store, glancing up and down the street. The sleeve of his shirt sported a rip. A swath of mud streaked his forehead. He'd never looked so handsome.

"Ethan!"

"Summer!" He hefted me into his arms. "Thank God you're all right."

"What are you doing here?"

"I came to take you to lunch. I took refuge under the overpass outside of town. When the tornado dissipated, I got here as fast as I could." He sat me on top of a car and ran his hands up and down my arms. "Are you hurt bad? We need to clean these cuts."

I shook my head. "I hid behind a Dumpster. We have to check on Sherry. She was inside the store."

"Okay. Stay here." Ethan rushed to where my car blocked the entrance to the store as effectively as a stopper in a bottle.

I slid from my perch and followed. Ethan tried the door, now unlocked but hanging crooked from its hinges. He rammed the door with his shoulder.

"Sherry! Can you hear me?" The door didn't open enough for a person to squeeze through.

"Can you climb over the car?" I studied my former mode of transportation. If Ethan climbed through the missing back window, over the backseat, and out the driver's side window, it might work.

"I'm not going to try that. The whole thing could come crashing down." He grabbed my hand and pulled me along as he ran down the street and through the alley I'd taken refuge in, before stopping at the back entrance to the store.

He tried the knob. The door squeaked open. "Will you stay out here?"

I shook my head. "She might need me." The adrenaline wore off, and I shivered, huddling close to Ethan's back.

"We don't usually get tornadoes in September."

"Not in quite a few years, but it's been known to happen. We had one when my dad was a kid. An F3. This one just sideswiped us." He ran his gaze over me. "Are you sure you're all right?"

"I'm cold."

He pulled his polo shirt over his head and

slipped it over mine, leaving him in a white sleeveless undershirt. Still warm from his body, heat from the cotton fabric seeped through me. I followed him through the dark room to where we could see the crinkled hood of my car.

"She'd been hiding over there." I pointed to the corner where I'd last seen Sherry.

It was empty.

26

We searched the entire store, Aunt Eunice." I leaned against the kitchen counter and chased down a couple of aspirin with a glass of water. "Where could she have gone?"

"I guess the twister might have sucked her out and deposited her in the next county." Aunt Eunice soaked a rag in warm water from the sink and handed it to Ethan, who took my arm in his hands and gently wiped away the blood.

I hissed against the sting. He smiled at me from beneath lowered lashes then blew on the scrapes. Tingles ran up my spine. Clever man. He knew just how to take my mind off my aches and pains. "I'm serious."

"I'm sorry. I shouldn't crack jokes, not even about Sherry."

Uncle Roy stomped into the kitchen. "Ain't hide nor hair of the woman. That Sonata of Summer's had the store window effectively clogged. No way in or out but through the back door or through the car itself. I took a quick peek but didn't do a thorough search of the place. Not many places a woman of her size could hide."

He plopped into a chair. "Do y'all think she's wandering town aimlessly, having lost her mind? Maybe she was hit in the head."

A month ago, Big Foot roamed our backyard. Now, Sherry wandered through town with a simple mind. Sometimes, Uncle Roy's imagination overruled his common sense.

"I'll call the hospitals," Aunt Eunice offered. "Maybe somebody turned her in."

"She isn't a lost dog." The aspirin did nothing for my headache. How long did the little white tablets take anyway?

Maybe Ethan could blow on my forehead. I glanced at my watch. Five minutes! No wonder my head still pounded. I forced my mind back to the issue at hand.

We knew nothing about Sherry. Did she have any family? How long had she lived in Mountain Shadows? She'd seemed so happy when I'd glimpsed her through the store window.

Before the tornado. For the first time since I'd met her, her face hadn't been twisted by a frown. Was she lying injured in a ditch?

Finished with the cloth, Ethan moved me to a chair and stepped behind me to massage my shoulders. He paused long enough to plant a soft kiss on the nape of my neck. And to think I tried running away from him. How could I even think about returning such a gift as precious as his love?

"Has anyone called to report her missing?" My head fell forward under Ethan's ministrations.

"I did. Joe's sending an officer to ask around

town." Uncle Roy waved for Aunt Eunice to refill his coffee. "He said he'd keep us informed, but they really can't consider her missing until tomorrow. I hope Mae Belle had insurance on that store. There's quite a bit of damage."

Great. One more thing I had to deal with. I straightened. "I need to get over to the candy store."

Ethan held me in place. "Tomorrow will be fine. Nothing's going to change overnight."

"I took a peek inside when I was in town," Uncle Roy said. "Besides the shattered front window and some water from the rain, doesn't look too bad. I bet you won't lose much more than a few boxes of candy. Mae Belle's place, well, that's another story."

He removed his baseball cap and rubbed his head. "Funny thing is, Mountain Shadows only got sideswiped by that twister. How'd your car end up where it is?" He replaced his cap. "Unless someone tried driving it and lost control."

"I thought that strange, too." Ethan's hands stilled. "Why would someone leave a building and come outside to steal a car during a twister?"

Uh-oh. I'd left my key in the ignition before dashing down the alley. Chalk up another point to Summer's quick thinking. And so much for selling A Dream Wedding.

I'd probably benefit more from closing the place down and taking the insurance money. Besides, now with Sherry missing, I had no one to run the business anyway.

I didn't really believe the twister had sucked her out the window. The woman disappeared, either out of fear for her safety, or something more sinister.

After Uncle Roy's comment, I suspected she'd tried to take my car. I made a mental note to do everything I could to find her. Just because I'd let her stay on at A Dream Wedding didn't mean I trusted her.

The sky outside the kitchen window brightened as the last of the storm clouds blew past. Headache subsiding, and hours left before nightfall, I was raring to go. I tilted my head back to glance at Ethan. "Will you take me back to town?"

"You sure you feel up to it? You got beaten up pretty bad back there."

I nodded. "Minor scrapes and bruises. I've had worse. We can tape plastic over the candy store window while we're in town."

"Okay. Roy, do you have any plastic?"

"I've got some drop cloths left from when I painted the front room. But plywood would be better. It'll keep looters out. I'll get you some. Be right back." He heaved his bulk from the chair and headed out back to his shed.

"Y'all should've nailed the windows before bringing me home." I leaned into Ethan.

"You first, Tink. Besides, who'd want to steal a bunch of candy?"

***

Traffic was scarce between home and Mountain Shadows, but Main Street bustled. Tow trucks moved cars. Volunteers righted upended trash cans. Store owners swept sidewalks.

Hammers pounded nails in doors. My car still poked its rear from the front of A Dream Wedding.

"Stop." I put a hand on Ethan's arm. "Sherry worked for Mae Belle, so there should be a job application with her home address. I want to see if I can locate it, then we can go by her home and see if she's all right."

"Sounds like a plan."

Ethan steered his truck down the alley and parked behind the store. No longer suffering from the shock of having survived a twister while huddled in a stairwell, I noticed the destruction inside. Doors blown open had left papers, mixed with garbage from outside, swirled from one room to the next.

Finding something with an address could be next to impossible. I prayed for a small miracle.

"Well, now would be a good time to redecorate." Ethan grinned.

"What, you don't like pink and white?"

"Not in this volume. I'll take the front. You take the office. It doesn't look as bad. I poked my head in when we were looking for Sherry earlier. You won't have to dig through pieces of glass."

I nodded and shoved against the office door. A few strong pushes and I'd managed to move aside the chair blocking my entrance.

Besides looking as if a child had picked up the room and shaken it, things weren't too bad. The desk sat skewed in a corner. Chairs lay on their sides, and a file cabinet lay dented on the floor, manila folders peeking from partially opened drawers.

Thank You, God. This should be easy. I righted the furniture on my way to thumb through the files.

Mae Belle had been optimistic. Most of the folders were empty, waiting to be filled.

The sight saddened me. Despite being disliked, Mae Belle was now dead and had no chance of filling those empty files. Mixed in with the files of her few clients, one folder said *Sherry Grover* on a pink-colored tab.

I grabbed it. I opened the file on top of the desk. From the address, I knew Sherry lived a couple of blocks away. Someone, possibly Mae Belle, had put a large question mark beside Sherry's name.

Was my cousin questioning the identity of her employee? Or just where she lived? I shook my head.

Since I took it upon myself to solve mysteries, I now seemed to try to find falsehoods in everything.

"I've got it!" I called. I could hear Ethan crunching over glass as he made his way back to me.

"Wow. A lot of damage for a room in the back of the store. Looks like someone might have been searching for something."

His brows drew together in a frown. "I took a look at your car." He dangled my keys in front of my face. "Did you leave these inside?"

"Yeah." My face heated. "I started to drive home, saw the twister, and ran away instead." I gave him a sheepish smile. "I kind of hoped no one would find out."

A dimple winked from his right cheek. "Come on, brave Tinkerbell. Let's pay a visit to Sherry." He held out his hand, and I took it.

Inside the truck, I handed Ethan the folder. He

glanced at the address. "I know where this is. It's an apartment over the antique store." He turned his key in the ignition.

After hammering plywood over the window of Summer Confections, we stood and stared at the back of the building housing Sherry's apartment. No cars in the carport.

Shuttered windows looked out over the alley entrance. Nothing appeared as if a tornado had blown through a couple of hours ago. "Well, we won't know anything if we don't knock." I led the way up the steep flight of stairs.

The wood-paneled door opened at my touch. "Hello? Sherry?"

"Let me go first." Ethan stepped in front of me and handed me his cell phone. "If anything happens, get out of here and call Joe immediately."

Little light penetrated the cracks of the wood shutters. Inside the apartment looked like it had been the center of the afternoon's storm. Clothes were strewed over every piece of furniture. Mail stacked high on the kitchen table. Dishes piled in the sink. My heart thudded painfully.

"Unless she's content to live like a pig, it doesn't look as if anyone has been here in a while." I tightened my hold on Ethan's phone.

"Let's check the bedroom."

Blankets hung off the bed. The closet door hung open, empty. A few articles of clothing lay on the floor. We stepped into the bathroom. The medicine cabinet was also empty.

No toothbrush or toothpaste lay beside the sink. Knowing my past of finding bodies in the shower, I held my breath and ripped aside the curtain. Nothing.

I took a deep breath. "I don't think Sherry's coming back."

27

Monday morning, Aunt Eunice and I cleaned up the mess from Sunday's storm. Uncle Roy had been right. Shattered glass and rain covered the tiled floor. A few soggy boxes of candy were the extent of the damage inside Summer Confections.

We'd reported Sherry missing, and the Mountain Shadows Police Department, humble as it may be, had added her to their list of things to take care of. They definitely needed my help.

As I swept and Aunt Eunice wiped dusty counters, I ran the never-ending list of questions through my mind. How could I interview my suspects again? I had absolutely no desire to visit the dentist to drill him more while I sat at the mercy of his tools of death. Edna and I didn't run in the same social circles any more than Mason and I did. Since there were no impending funerals, I had no reason to visit the funeral parlor or have an excuse to go to Larry Bell's farm. I'd hit a dead end and saw no path to continue.

"Why the long face, Summer?" Aunt Eunice

stacked some dry boxes near the counter.

I explained my frustration. "You'll have to get creative. Why not throw a barbecue?"

"On what grounds?" I dumped the glass from the dustpan into the garbage. "I can't just call up my suspect list and invite them over for hot dogs."

A mental light bulb exploded over my head. "Your anniversary is coming up. We can throw a party and invite just about everyone."

Aunt Eunice pursed her lips. "The only one who might be suspicious would be Mason White. He'll wonder why we're inviting him. But it's worth a try. The man probably won't come after what happened to Renee."

"We'll invite him in reciprocation of his party, and tell him the chance to get out will cheer him up." The idea took root and grew at an alarming rate. "And since Joe is family, he'll be there as security in case someone takes offense to our nosiness. He can't get mad if we question people in our own home. Can he?"

"I don't see how. Let's do it this weekend. You stay here and make party mints. Pink, green, and yellow ones. I'll go home and work on the guest list after I stop at the party store to get invitations." She clapped her hands.

"This will be so much fun. We'll have games and dancing. I'll get Roy to call his music buddies from the lodge. Then we can head over to the warehouse store later for the food." Aunt Eunice practically skipped out the door.

Party mints, huh? I set aside my broom and put white chocolate on the burner to melt. They'd take me all day to make.

Once the chocolate melted, I added flavoring and, using a funnel, made coin-sized, pastel-colored discs on wax paper.

The bell over the door jangled.

I lifted my head as Mason approached the counter. I propped the funnel over the pan of remaining chocolate and wiped my hands.

"Welcome, Mason." I pasted a smile on my face and approached him, keeping the counter safely between us. Handsome or not, the guy scared me.

"Summer." His gaze pierced me, raking over the red ruffled apron I wore. "You're looking. . .quite fetching." He shook his head. "Look, all fun and games aside. I need your help."

"Help?" My voice squeaked.

"I want you to find out who killed Renee."

Like I wasn't trying to already? "Why me? Why don't you go to the police? You've always made fun of me before."

He gnawed his lower lip. "It's. . .delicate."

"Some people think you may have killed her. She died at your house, during your party. And delicate or not, Mason, your relationship with Renee isn't exactly a secret."

He shrugged, and his lip curled into a sneer. "I'm a smart aleck, Summer. Not a murderer."

Yeah, well. Richard Bland, the guy I'd helped capture, and inadvertently killed a few months ago, remained fresh in my mind. He'd been a gentleman, a diamond thief, *and* a murderer.

"Uh, I'm throwing an anniversary party for my aunt and uncle on Saturday. A lot of people will be there. Why don't you come and snoop around?"

He smiled. "I'll do that." Mason chucked me under the chin. "Save a dance for me, won't you?" He spun around and strolled out the door.

Puh-leese! I rubbed his touch off my face. I ought to tell Ethan so he could knock the guy out. I didn't believe Mason was a murderer either, but I wasn't going to remove him from my list just yet.

I turned back to my candy. For someone who professed to be grieving over a loved one, Mason still found the time to flirt with me.

Almost the end of September and I'd be getting married on April Fool's Day. Less than seven months away, and I'd done nothing but rip out pictures of what I wanted because I'd been silly enough to hire my cousin as a wedding planner.

Most people took a year or more to plan their special day. With a mystery to solve, when would I find the time?

I sighed again as the bell announced another customer. A smile broke out when Ethan strolled through the door and back to where I worked. "Hungry?"

"Aunt Eunice left. I can't leave the store."

He bent over and kissed me. "I'm on my prep time. I'll bring lunch to you. The usual?" I nodded.

As quick as he arrived, he was gone. When he returned with fat, juicy hamburgers and salty French fries, I pulled a couple of stools to the packing table and filled him in on the weekend's plans. He stared at me over his burger. "Okay. I'll be near you the entire time. Ask all the questions you want, and I'll be your bodyguard. Maybe I'll catch something you don't."

Never in a million years would I have thought Ethan would be my sidekick in the crime-solving business. At first, I'd pictured April, but she'd gotten wrapped up in Joe. Then Aunt Eunice just naturally filled the vacant position. I learned a few weeks ago that Ethan was much nicer to have

along on a stakeout. His kisses kept me warm.

"That will be wonderful." Again, I entertained thoughts of opening a detective agency titled "Banning Investigations."

***

By the weekend, Uncle Roy had laid planks of wood across the uneven ground making a dance floor of sorts. From the trees, he strung strands of white Christmas lights. Other than that, the prevalent color was gold.

Everywhere. Tables, candles, dishes, streamers. The back lawn looked as if a leprechaun had upended his treasured pot. The air cried with the tuning of musical instruments.

"Isn't it beautiful?" Aunt Eunice bustled past, her arms loaded with a large dish of potato salad.

"Very bright. I need my sunglasses."

"Could you get Ethan to start a fire in the pit? The night might get chilly, and the guests will be arriving any time now."

"Okay." I turned and went in search of my sidekick. I found him on the front porch laughing with Joe. After sending the two of them off to do Aunt Eunice's bidding, I took Ethan's seat on the rocking chair and watched the guests arrive.

Townspeople, neighbors, and friends arrived in

jovial moods, bearing gifts in gold or white paper. Mason sped into the yard, followed closely by a white van. From the back of the van, two men rolled an ice sculpture in the shape of two swans, their necks entwined.

In spite of the man's generous donation, I hoped it contained sparkling cider rather than champagne. Uncle Roy wouldn't allow alcohol anywhere near his house, and his grumbling wouldn't be helpful in keeping the guests in a good mood.

Mason approached the porch. "May I speak with you, Summer?"

I rose and followed him around the corner. "The fountain is a token of my appreciation for you helping me locate Renee's murderer." Mason held up a hand to stop my protests. "I realize you aren't really a detective, but with your reputation of being in the right place at the wrong time, I have no doubt you'll find out who's behind this." He grinned. "And now, I'll go do my part and mingle."

I stared at his retreating back.

"What is he talking about?" Joe joined me. "Eavesdropping, dear cousin?"

"Yes. What have you cooked up with Mason?"

"I'm helping him locate Renee's killer. And, in doing so, will probably find Mae Belle's."

He raised his eyebrows. "Mason is a suspect."

"I know. And he'll be easier to keep an eye on if he's underfoot." I crossed my arms. "I'm not a complete idiot."

"As opposed to half of one?" He grabbed my arm and dragged me farther from the house. "What does Ethan think of this scheme of yours?"

"He'll be by my side the entire evening." I jerked free of his grasp.

"Like he is now?"

"There's no need when I have such a brave officer of the law concerned with my welfare, now is there? There are close to a hundred people here. I think I'm safe enough." Would Joe ever let me grow up?

"It's easier to disappear in a crowd."

220

28

Fire's roaring, music's playing, and I've got a pretty girl in my arms. What more could a guy ask for?" Ethan twirled me around the makeshift dance floor.

"How about an end to this case so I can plan our wedding?" I glanced at the dancers around us. Uncle Roy spun Aunt Eunice, Joe waltzed with April, the good dentist,

Hubert, moved with Edna, and Mason sped by with a pretty girl I hadn't met. Others danced in a kaleidoscope of color.

Ethan pulled me closer. "Most of the town is here. At least everyone who'd be on our guest list. We could get married now then run off to some exotic place for our honeymoon."

I pulled back far enough to gaze into his face. "Don't tempt me. And I *expect* a honeymoon to remember." My cheeks heated. Not that I knew a lot about what to expect.

Aunt Eunice tried giving me "the talk" when I started high school, but she stammered and stuttered so much that I had to find out the facts myself, through books. And the heart-pounding,

breath-stealing nature of Ethan's kisses.

The song ended, and the band struck up a square dance. "Let's sit this one out. Unless you want your feet pounded to a pulp." Ethan led me to the sparkling cider fountain. Ruby and Mabel, Aunt Eunice's best friends, approached and held plastic champagne glasses beneath the pale amber flow.

"Summer, there aren't enough eligible men at this party." Ruby raised her drink.

"It's an anniversary party. Not a place to pick up men." I smiled at Ethan.

"I know." Ruby nodded. "That's what church is for."

Ethan sputtered, spraying the area around us with his drink.

"Really, Ethan." Mabel frowned. "I thought your parents taught you better manners." She wiggled a finger at me. "And you. Don't give us any story about an anniversary party. Granted, it serves that purpose, but Eunice already told us you're scoping out your cousin's killer."

And Renee's. Was nothing secret in this town? "Please, don't talk about it. I don't want this to be Mountain Shadows' main topic of conversation for the next several weeks."

"Mum's the word, right, Mabel?" Ruby raised her glass.

"Right." They linked arms and trotted away, chattering about the excitement of being in on a dangerous secret. I shook my head. Next thing I knew, it'd be in the local paper.

Ethan nuzzled my neck. "Want to neck in the woods?"

"Stop." I pushed him away and giggled. We've got to focus. This entire thing is a fiasco. I'm surprised the killer doesn't walk up, put a gun to my head, and pull the trigger just to stop my nosing around." Someone tapped my shoulder.

I jumped and screamed. Ethan snorted.

"Why are you so skittish? And why are you flushed? Are you getting sick?" Aunt Eunice wiped a napkin across her shining brow. "That last dance wore me out. Find any information?"

"No."

"And you won't either, hiding over here. You've got to mingle, girl. Ethan, pull her way from the cider and get her out there."

"Yes, ma'am." He wrapped his arm around my waist and led me toward the buffet table.

Movement to our right caught my eye. Hubert and Edna sneaked into the shadows of the trees behind the house. She giggled up at him.

"Let's spy." I tugged on Ethan's hand. "Maybe we'll learn something."

"I don't think you want to be caught watching what those two have planned." He popped an olive into his mouth.

"Oh." My face heated. "They're sneaking off like a couple of teenagers. They've both got to be approaching sixty."

"I hope we're that frisky when we're sixty." He planted a quick kiss on my lips and tickled my sides until I shrieked.

"Still looking for clues, I see." Aunt Eunice glared at us from across the table.

I pulled free of Ethan's embrace. "Stop sneaking up on me, Aunt Eunice. We can't be obvious about our snooping. And contrary to what you believe, I'm paying attention."

I leaned against the table, crossed my arms, and looked over the crowd. "Hubert and Edna disappeared into the woods. Oh look, they're coming back. That was fast.

Larry Bell glares at everyone from the dessert table, and Mason doesn't appear heartbroken as he flirts with all the pretty girls. Then there's Lewis Anderson pretending to be attentive to his wife. Have I missed anyone on our list? Besides Sherry, that is?"

Aunt Eunice humphed and stalked away.

I sighed. "We probably should start up conversations with everyone. We're not learning a thing here."

"No, but we're having more fun. Where do you want to start?"

"I don't even know *how* to start." I allowed my gaze to roam the crowd again. Larry had disappeared, the lovebirds were again nestled out of sight, and Mason strolled toward us.

"I guess we start with Mason."

Mason downed a glass of cider and reached for another before acknowledging our presence. "Champagne would hit the spot better."

"Cider doesn't seem to be hurting you any." I glared at him. "I thought you were distraught over Renee's death." Ethan elbowed me.

"I am." Mason tossed his cup in a nearby trash can.

"That's why I asked you to check around for me. I'm not doing anything but mingling."

"Looking for your next conquest is more like it."

Mason laughed. "Ethan, your girl is a real trip. But she's barking up the wrong tree." He leaned closer to us. "See that man over there? The one in jeans? He just arrived to the party. That's Bill Olson, Renee's fiancé. Seems he arrived home the day *before* my party. Makes you wonder, doesn't it? You might want to check *him* out. Renee said he was really mad. And that's my cue to leave." He winked and stalked away.

I studied the man searching the dance floor. Easily Ethan's height of six foot two inches, the biceps on Bill's arms were as big around as my thighs. Granted I was thin, but the man was still impressive, and I had no doubt who he looked for.

Ethan put a hand around my arm and guided me to Bill. "Bill." Ethan held out a hand. "Good to see you home."

The man turned red-rimmed, hazel eyes to us. Anger radiated from him in waves so intense, I should have worn sunscreen. "Not quite the homecoming I'd envisioned." Bill's muscles quivered. A muscle ticked in his jaw. "Where's the scumbag you were talking to? I'm going to kill him."

Ethan placed his hand on Bill's arm. "Don't do anything rash. Renee's death was—"

Bill shoved Ethan away. "Don't tell me it was an accident! She was murdered. Plain and simple. Lured away by that slime's silky tongue and sweet words."

"Bathroom," I blurted. "Yeah. He asked where the restroom was." *Great answer, Summer. Brilliant.* Another suspect just entered the mix. I felt like a hamster on a never-ending run around a stationary wheel. One watched closely by an enraged cat.

Ethan frowned, and I transferred my attention from the exasperated man next to me back to the safer task of studying the party guests. As the night wore on, groups huddled around what desserts remained, couples danced a little closer, and my suspects moved in separate directions.

Hubert headed to the house, apparently having lost Edna somewhere along the way. Larry had stopped glaring at the dance floor and marched toward the kitchen door. Aunt Eunice hooted with laughter at something Uncle Roy said.

The band played a lively, toe-tapping tune. Behind me, Bill's voice continued to rise. I strongly suspected the man had been drinking before he arrived.

Aunt Eunice and Uncle Roy danced a lively jig around the dance floor. Hubert popped his head out the kitchen door, glanced around, then withdrew. Anderson had disappeared, while his family huddled around the food table. Larry Bell marched from around the house, crossed his arms, glared, and leaned against the wooden siding.

I grinned, pleased with myself. I'd managed to keep tabs on all my suspects, mostly. I sipped from the cup I still held.

They'd all drifted in and out of my line of fire during the evening but were mostly accounted for. I was getting good at this.

A woman screamed.

Ethan grabbed my hand and dashed toward the sound. A crowd had gathered on the opposite side of Uncle Roy's shed. A woman's legs hung over the side of a barrel used to collect rainwater. Her head disappeared in the murky depths.

Joe ordered everyone to step aside and did what should have been done minutes ago. He pulled the woman from the water. Edna's pale face stared at us with bulging, lifeless eyes.

A scrap of paper fluttered from the bodice of her gown. I reached for it and read.

Ladies first.

228

29

Joe barked orders for the onlookers to move back then shouted into the cell phone he whipped from his pocket. His long strides carried him from behind the shed to the middle of the lawn.

Ethan did his best to keep the crowd contained until help could arrive, Aunt Eunice clutched Uncle Roy's arm, April plopped to the ground, and I scanned the horrified faces around me.

No Mason, Bill, Hubert, or Larry. I wasn't surprised.

I glanced back at the paper in my hand. The words were cut from a magazine. Just like the threatening note I'd received. *Ladies first?* I gnawed my lip.

Mae Belle and Lewis. Renee and Mason. Edna and Hubert. All couples cut down to half. All unmarried.

A shiver ran down my spine. What about me and April? We were single, female, and part of a couple. Was the killer now going to concentrate on the men?

"Edna?" Hubert called from the back porch. "Ready or not, here I come!"

A heavy silence came over the crowd as we all turned, in sync, to where Hubert's form was backlit by the kitchen window. Uncle Roy gently removed my aunt's hands from his arm and made his way to where Hubert laughed. Seconds later, the man sagged sobbing into my uncle's arms.

Mason appeared around the corner at a fast trot, Bill on his heels. Both men stopped suddenly and glanced from us to the two men on the porch. "Truce." Mason's word drifted to where I stood.

"Everyone stay put." Joe slipped his phone into the pocket of his jeans. "You'll all be questioned, and it's going to take a while. Break it up, get something to eat, but don't leave."

He grabbed my arm and dragged me to the side. "I know you've been snooping around tonight. Aunt Eunice told me of your plans. Did you see or hear anything?"

I handed him the note. "I found this on the ground after you pulled Edna from the water. I can't vouch for the whereabouts of all the guests. I was only trying to keep tabs on my suspect list, all of whom were out of my sight for at least a few minutes during the time of Edna's drowning. But not for long. It must've been fast."

"It was. She's still—"

"I don't want to hear it." I shuddered. "Someone seems to be murdering the feminine half of a couple. I've got to admit I'm quite freaked out here. I'm part of a couple. So are you and April and my aunt and uncle."

I clutched at him. "There's something we're missing, Joe. Something simple. I feel it. It's right there, at the edge of my mind, but I can't pull it out."

"Work on it. I'll get your aunt and April. I want the three of you to stay together." He put his face so close to mine I thought our noses would touch. "I mean it. If one of you goes to the bathroom, the other two go. I'll send Ethan for you once I no longer need him."

"You're scaring me. Ethan isn't a cop. Why can't I have him now?"

Joe's eyes narrowed. "You should be scared, and with a crowd this size, I need all the help I can get. I've called for backup, but these people will listen to Ethan. They like him."

He dragged me to Aunt Eunice then went to get April. I craned my neck looking for Ethan. He still worked crowd control. My body relaxed with the first wail of an approaching siren.

"We need to get closer. I want to hear when the cops question people. Who found the body?"

"Ruby and Mabel." Aunt Eunice hugged herself. "They said they were just walking around, gossiping like they do, and found her upside down, white undies shining in the

moonlight. What an awful way to go." She wiped her eyes with the corner of her sleeve. "No dignity."

"Once the cops get here," April explained upon joining us, "they'll each take different people to question. How are you supposed to guarantee you'll hear the ones you want?"

"Well. . ." Good question. There wasn't time, or enough of us, to listen to every person being interrogated. I stood on my tiptoes to try and see over the crowd. "I'd like to hear Mason, Bill, Larry, and Hubert."

I sat on a cement block and rested my chin in my hand. "You're right. I don't even know where they are."

"Don't give up." Aunt Eunice popped me on the head.

"Joe just said we had to stay together. He didn't say we had to stay in this exact spot. They'll be taking people into the house. You know how thin these old walls are. I know the perfect place, but we've got to hurry. If we're spotted, especially by your uncle, they'll stop us."

April and I glanced at each other then hurried to follow a bustling Aunt Eunice. "Come on," she ordered. "Help me pull up this door."

She'd taken us to the storm cellar. I could've slapped myself in the forehead. There was no better spot in the entire house than beneath it.

The door led to a basement complete with a furnace that had made it impossible for me to have the courage to enter here as a child. But more importantly, there were floor vents in every room, giving access to the heat. We'd be able to hear whatever we wanted from every downstairs room. We could listen in on the interrogations from the kitchen, living, and dining rooms.

"God bless old homes. Aunt Eunice, you're a genius." I tugged on the heavy wooden square. Aunt Eunice hissed a warning to be quiet when it slammed open. "If we can hear them, they'll be able to hear us. For once, I'm glad we haven't renovated this basement or modernized our heating."

She peered around us and scuttled down the stairs. I climbed down last, closing the door and casting us into darkness except for stenciled squares of light coming from the ornate metal vents.

"We'll each take a room. Give a heads-up if you hear anything interesting," Aunt Eunice whispered.

Dust rained down on us as feet marched overhead.

"This is ridiculous!" a male voice said.

"That's Mason!" I pointed over our heads.

Aunt Eunice held a finger to her lips.

"Come on, Joe, you can't actually believe I did in that old lady!" A chair creaked. "I didn't even know her."

"We're questioning everyone, Mason. Got a guilty conscience?"

"I've heard the whispering. I was in attendance at Renee's death, and now this one. Of course everyone is pointing at me. Want to know what I think? Bill Olson. Man's mad enough to do just about anything. He actually threatened me. Said he was going to kill me."

"Guess you'd better watch your back then."

"Are you judging me? Aren't you going to do anything? I'm a taxpayer. I deserve protection."

"I could put you in protective custody." I could just picture Joe, crossing his arms and leaning back in his chair.

"Just get on with the questions, chief." Joe had obviously touched on a nerve. Mason switched from first names to using professional titles.

"When you left the dance floor, you went where?"

"To the house. I was trying to get away from Bill Olson. I stayed there until I heard the woman scream. Ran out, ran into Bill, and now here I am."

"Can anyone verify that?"

"Let's cut to the chase. I know how this works. There's about twenty minutes where I was alone. I've got no concrete alibi."

I wasn't going to find out anything from Mason. I shuffled to Aunt Eunice. "Who've you got?"

"Larry Bell. Very boring. He sounds like a broken record. Name, date, and he's asking for a lawyer. Seems he's got no one to vouch for him."

April joined us. "They couldn't get a thing out of Hubert. All the man did was cry. Now they're talking to Ruby and Mabel." She crossed her arms. "Can we go now? I'm getting cold."

I couldn't help feeling let down. I'd stake the candy store that someone from the party killed Edna. It wouldn't be someone sneaking in from the woods. Too convenient. Still, it didn't seem planned. Had the killer just seen an opportunity and taken it?

We stepped from the inky darkness of the basement into a star-filled night. The backyard looked like a glittery wonderland overshadowed by a cloud of death trimmed with castoff gold decorations.

Ethan and a police officer kept the guests in a line and filed them through the house like sheep to be questioned. Lewis Anderson fidgeted and kept glancing at his watch. His wife, a plump, harried-looking woman, did her best to keep two bored teenage boys under control.

"Why doesn't Joe just send everyone home and take down their names?" Aunt Eunice glared at April. "This is going to take half the night, and I've still got to clean up."

"I don't know. And don't give me that look. This wasn't my idea." April slumped next to me.

"We're all tired and getting testy. The murderer is here somewhere." I scanned the yard. "I'm sure Joe believes that, too. He'll question everyone, hoping to get lucky, and let the others go if they've got alibis. That's what I'd do." I led them to a table and took a seat, wrapping my arms around me to try and stay warm.

I'd taken everyone's advice and asked God to help me solve the case, but so far He wasn't answering. I sighed. Maybe it was me. I didn't slow down long enough to listen.

Bill Olson barged through the back door, stormed down the steps, kicked the garbage can, and marched away. His interview obviously didn't go well. I turned to my aunt.

"Did Joe say anything against our waiting in the house? Maybe there's an empty room we can wait in. At least we'll be warm." I shivered.

But there was an officer stationed at each door, and neither would grant us entry. Frustrated, we headed to my aunt's truck and sat in the dark staring at the house. They'd have to question us, too.

I settled in for a long wait. Within minutes, Aunt Eunice's head rested on my shoulder and snores emanated from her mouth. April rustled around on the other side of Aunt Eunice and eventually grew silent.

At regular intervals someone would exit the front of the house, climb behind the wheel of their car, and drive away. The night wound down. My eyelids grew heavy, and I slumped against the driver's side door.

It creaked open. I flung out an arm to keep from falling and found myself staring into a black abyss where a face should have been.

30

The wraith reached for me with skeletal hands. Okay, human hands but every bit as frightening. I leaned back against Aunt Eunice and kicked, pedaling with both legs.

April screamed loud enough to bust the windows. The door slammed as she escaped out the other side.

Aunt Eunice bent over me, flailing her arms in an attempt to punch the silent attacker. "In the name of Jesus! Be gone! Be gone! Angels protect us. Heaven help us!"

Red eyes glowed from beneath the hood. *Red eyes?*

When its hands closed on my ankles, it felt like ice shackles burning into my skin. A nightmare from hades come to torment me. The evil monster from every horror movie I'd watched without permission as a child. Why hadn't I listened to my elders and stayed in bed? Too many times, I'd sneaked downstairs after my aunt and uncle were in bed and huddled in front of the television.

The *thing* pulled and dragged me by the feet from the truck. My head bounced off the seat, banged against the rim around the door, and I landed with a jolt on the gravel driveway. The air left my lungs in a painful *whoosh*.

The demon continued to drag me over the gravel drive. Rocks sliced into my hands as I fought to grab. . .anything.

Small as I was, I never considered myself weak. I'd always compared myself to Mighty Mouse, but this silent aggressor hauled me as if I weighed nothing. My heart lodged in my throat. I locked onto the shape of my aunt's face as a safety anchor.

My shrieks joined Aunt Eunice and April. Aunt Eunice launched herself toward my attacker, missed, and fell with a cry to the ground. She pushed to one elbow and pointed. "Unmask yourself. Show your face like a man."

Then, like the phantom it resembled, the black-shrouded figure disappeared.

"Hey!" Ethan sprinted toward us. Sparing a glance to the departing attacker, he helped me rise. "Are you all right?"

"I'm—fine. Other—than having—a heart attack." My breath shuddered. *Get a grip, Summer.* "Go after him. If you catch him, we'll have solved our mystery." I grabbed his hand and tugged.

"Summer, you're bleeding. You're scraped. We aren't going anywhere."

"My hands are cut, too." Aunt Eunice held them up from her position on the ground. Ethan pulled her to her feet.

He cast one more glance to where the phantom disappeared into the trees. Desire to give chase clearly fought with staying to care for us. Ethan sighed. "Come on, ladies. Let's get you cleaned up. April, you can stop hiding now."

She poked her head around the front of the truck. "I wasn't. I was getting ready to run for help, but Joe told us to stay together."

"Good thing we did." Aunt Eunice straightened her shirt. "If I wasn't here to save Summer, she'd be a goner for sure. April just screeched like a cat who'd got its tail stuck in the screen door."

"I think I handled myself pretty well, considering the attacker woke me," I mumbled. Except for the freaking-out part and reliving a nightmare.

When my adrenaline subsided, my hands stung. Small pebbles were embedded in my palms. The bone at the base of my spine ached, and I knew I'd be walking like an old crone for the next few hours. I lifted a hand and winced at a bump rising on the back of my head.

Ethan herded us toward the house and into the kitchen. "The officers finished questioning everyone, and I had headed outside to look for you when I heard the screaming." He turned on the faucet and stuck my hands beneath the flow.

"Joe's going to be—"

"What?" Joe entered the room. "I'm going to be what?"

"Livid," I answered. "The three of us stayed together like you told us and took refuge in Aunt

Eunice's truck to stay warm because your officers wouldn't let us come in the house."

The water soothed my scraped hands. "Someone dressed in a black, ghost-looking robe thing dragged me out. A wraith, I think. I'm lucky to be alive, you know."

Joe's mouth gaped. "Right under my nose? With police officers in the house?"

"He's either brave or foolish." Aunt Eunice took my place by the sink. "I'm pretty positive it was a man. I know they wore a robe, but there weren't any, uh, you know—up top."

Ethan's eyes widened. A dimple winked in his cheek.

Joe's face reddened. "Good grief, Aunt Eunice."

"I'm just telling you what I noticed." She dried her hands on a clean towel. "It helps, doesn't it? Knowing you can rule out women from your suspect list?"

"Did *you* notice anything?" Joe turned to me.

"I was too busy trying to survive, but, considering the strength in those hands, I'd say it's a man. In a Halloween costume. He didn't seem to have a face, and the eyes were red."

"Of course it's a costume!" Joe rubbed his head. "Wraiths don't roam the streets of Mountain Shadows. Especially without a face. The killer must be getting desperate to attempt abducting Summer with people around."

"Everyone was in the house. Except for the three of us in the truck. And we were sleeping." I gasped. "Maybe he meant to sedate me, but I woke up too soon."

Uncle Roy bolted in to join us and rushed to Aunt Eunice's side. "Are you hurt? Did we catch 'em? Do I need my gun?"

"We could've used it a bit ago. Almost lost our lives to that killer who likes to split up couples. And, no, he got away." Aunt Eunice laid her head on his chest. Uncle Roy wrapped his arms around her and murmured.

"I'm going to make coffee." April reached for the pot, apparently realizing she could actually be useful.

I mentally chastised myself. She couldn't be blamed for going all paranoid. The faceless wraith shook me up, too. I smiled. "That would be great."

Joe ducked into the hall for a minute and returned with an older officer sporting a salt-and-pepper crew cut. "This is Officer McHale. He's going to take notes so we can make sense of this madness. Summer, you first." Joe pointed to a kitchen chair. "I need to know anything you might have gathered by snooping tonight."

"Nothing, really. Like I told you earlier, all my suspects were out of sight during the time Edna was murdered. The last person I saw her with was Hubert. Then he came outside still expecting to be playing some lovers' game of hide-and-seek. That could just be a ruse, of course. But"—I smiled a thank-you to April when she handed me a mug of coffee.

The warmth seeped into my aches—"Bill Olson's fired up. I think he knows about Renee's affair. Mason scattered as soon as he laid eyes on him. He could be angry enough to commit murder. Maybe Edna got in the way."

"My turn." Aunt Eunice practically shoved me from the chair to take my place. "I learned you don't take naps in an unlocked vehicle during a murder investigation." She crossed her arms. "I also learned that Larry Bell doesn't spill his guts when questioned, and that Hubert cries like a girl. No offense, he did just lose a loved one. When we eavesdropped from the cellar—"

She froze, her mouth forming a perfect *O*.

I rolled my eyes. The woman never could keep a secret.

Joe stabbed me with his gaze. I threw up my hands. "It wasn't my idea. I just wanted to gather info. Aunt Eunice suggested the basement."

Officer McHale's lips twitched. Very few people on the face of this planet escaped being entertained by a few minutes in the company of my family. I've often thought script writers should model a sitcom after us.

"The only thing we know for sure is that Sherry is missing and someone likes to send threatening letters with words cut from magazines." I lowered my face over my mug. I'd just remembered where I'd seen a stack of magazines. And not just one. Since my brain was on a roll, I wondered whether Sherry had a computer and an alias.

I glanced up to see Ethan watching me. It wouldn't take much for him to figure out I was up to something. Hopefully, he'd be willing to go with me, if for no other reason than to watch over me.

31

"**Do not steal.** Do not lie. Do not deceive one another.' Leviticus 19:11."

The pastor's words scraped across my spirit. I'd been trying. Honestly. I'd hardly skirted around any questions asked about my investigative plans. But, and it was a big but, I knew Ethan would be busy after church today with the men's luncheon. The perfect time for me to do more snooping.

Ethan's presence beside me confirmed my decision. I flipped over the church notes and wrote, "I'm going back to Sherry's apartment after church, okay? I think we missed something."

He grabbed the pen from my hand and answered, "Don't go alone."

"I won't. I'm also going to—"

Aunt Eunice tapped me on the shoulder and handed me a slip of paper. "Writing notes in church like a teenager. The two of you ought to be ashamed."

What did she think *she* was doing? *Not* passing notes?

Ethan winked and straightened in his seat. Right before the closing prayer, Ethan rose, whispered in my ear that he'd see me later, and left to finish preparations for the luncheon.

After the prayer, I grabbed Aunt Eunice's arm to prevent her from leaving. "I need you to go somewhere with me. Can you?"

"I guess so. Your uncle's staying for lunch. Where're we going?"

"Snooping."

She clapped her hands. "Wonderful. And thank the Lord, we're going in the daytime. I don't want any more black ghosts sneaking up on us."

We stopped at the coffee bar, loaded up on icy caffeine drinks, then slid into Aunt Eunice's truck. It wasn't until we were halfway to town that I realized I'd never told Ethan about my second destination. I'd text him.

I dug my cell phone from my purse and sent him a quick message. There. No deceit or lies. I was in the clear.

"Thank You, Lord." Aunt Eunice cut the truck's engine. "I was so afraid there'd be police tape around her apartment. I really didn't want to get arrested again."

"That was six weeks ago, and since Sherry hasn't been involved with a crime—that we know of—there wouldn't be any tape." I shoved open my door. "Come on."

We climbed the stairs and peered into the messy apartment. I leaned against the door and almost fell as it swung open, unlocked. Aunt Eunice and I exchanged surprised looks and stepped inside.

A sour odor greeted us. "Still doesn't look like she's been back. And who would have left the door unlocked?"

Aunt Eunice shrugged and pulled the neckline of her blouse over her nose. "I'm thinking something had to have happened to her."

"That's my thought." I led the way inside. "I'm looking for her computer."

"I'm going to clean up."

I stared at her. Was she nuts? "You can't. If something did happen to her, the police will need things left as they are for evidence."

"Like you aren't going to leave fingerprints on the computer?"

"I—" She was right. There was no way around it. Besides, I'd already been here once. "We won't touch anything except what's necessary."

"What are we looking for anyway?"

"Anything that might have to do with Mae Belle or Renee. Especially anything with the name Lola."

That stopped my aunt in her progression to the kitchen. "Who's that?"

"Larry Bell's Internet love."

"You think Sherry is Lola?"

"Maybe." The woman was involved somehow. I wasn't buying her earlier story of needing a job at A Dream Wedding.

Okay, maybe she needed a job, but no one was that obsessive over one. Then after I heard that Mae Belle knew about Larry's computer fling, I knew Sherry had to be involved, or at least the woman knew something.

Aunt Eunice bustled to the kitchen and slammed open cabinet doors. "Nothing here. Oh wait." She reached beneath the kitchen sink. "Here are some rubber gloves." She tossed me a pair. "Are you sure I can't do these dirty dishes? Or take out the garbage? The stench is making me sick."

"Just leave it alone, Aunt Eunice." I stretched the gloves over my hands and headed to the bedroom. Sure enough, a computer sat on a corner desk, the surface around it piled with papers.

"Aunt Eunice, come help me." I sent her to work reading through the mountain of paper while I tried to gain access to the computer.

Ding after ding announced my failure, and I felt an overwhelming urge to throw the monitor through the window. Why couldn't I have been a computer hacker?

Half an hour later Aunt Eunice gasped and tossed a sheet of paper on the bed. "My eyes are burning out of my head! We're supposed to be careful of what our eyes see, and mine are not meant to see that X-rated garbage."

Curious, I grabbed the paper. My face heated as I read the very intimate, and graphic, love letter from Lola to the man who made her heart beat faster. I dropped the note like it would burn me. "Oh boy."

"Got enough information? I'm not reading anymore." Aunt Eunice scooped the papers back in a pile and thrust them at me. "What now?"

"Well, it's not proof that Sherry is Lola, but it might be enough for Joe to dig deeper into her e-mails." Relief flooded through me after not being able to access Sherry's files. No telling what I would've wandered into.

I sat on the bed, my arms full of indecent proposals. Had Sherry tried escaping the twister in my car, lost control, wrecked, then run off?

My gut told me she'd been the one driving it during the storm. Or had someone taken her from the car after it crashed through the store? If she did have something on Mae Belle, what was it? Was she holding Mae Belle's fling with Lewis Anderson over my cousin's head?

Why? I sighed. The more answers I got, the more questions that arose.

I glanced at my watch. The men's lunch would be over soon. My next stop would have to wait another day. And with tomorrow being Monday, work would take up most of my time. I shrugged. If I couldn't solve Mae Belle's murder, maybe this pile of illicit material would give Joe and the other officers enough to head them in the right direction.

"Let's go." I stood. "We'll stop by the station. Joe's on duty, and we can get this trash out of our possession."

***

Joe set the papers in the center of his desk blotter and stared at me and Aunt Eunice with eyes the color of slate. I squirmed on the hard plastic chair. My cousin's cheeks were Arkansas Razorback red. Two burning spots of color high on his cheekbones. He chewed the inside of his mouth then sighed.

"Y'all read these, I suppose."

"Do they help?" I leaned forward. I couldn't tell if he was upset because we'd read them or because we'd exposed ourselves to the filth.

"They might. Gives us reason to think Sherry might be in danger and not just on vacation somewhere."

"You thought she took a trip?" Really. Country cops.

He shook his head. "No." His answer dripped sarcasm. "It was just a theory." Joe pushed a button on his phone. "Send McHale in here."

A few minutes later, the officer poked his head around the door. "You wanted to see me?"

Joe scribbled Sherry's address on a slip of paper and handed it to the officer. "I need you to confiscate the computer at this address. Then send it to someone who can find a way to access it. Grab any printed sheets lying around."

"Yes, sir." Officer McHale disappeared.

Joe turned his attention back to us. Summer, Aunt Eunice. Thank you for your help, but I'll take it from here. Three people are dead. One's missing, and someone tried grabbing you at the party. No more snooping, no more questioning, no more anything. Am I making myself clear?"

"Perfectly." I rose. Aunt Eunice followed. "But I can't promise, Joe. I'm on a new track. One of complete honesty. I can tell you that if I hear anything, you'll be the first to know." I shot him a quick grin and strode from his office.

"Are we going home now?" Aunt Eunice's eyes twinkled. "Or do you have something else up your sleeve?"

32

I hunched over the tray of unrolled strawberry creams and pouted as I rolled tablespoon-sized portions into balls. Lewis Anderson hadn't been at the funeral home when Aunt Eunice and I stopped by yesterday.

I called Joe early this morning, and he wouldn't tell whether he suspected Sherry of being Lola or not. If no one would cooperate, how could I solve this?

Any more trouble and Joe would be forced to call in the state police or the FBI. Then I'd definitely be out of the loop. I didn't think they'd wire me and use me as bait like in the past.

Pink balls of candy lined the tray. My hands worked quickly while my mind raced. Speaking of the state police, why hadn't Joe called them in already? Did my cousin believe he was getting somewhere on the case? Did he think he could take care of things on his own?

Was he withholding information from me? I frowned and rolled my head on my shoulders. With this being my third mystery, I expected at least a small amount of professional courtesy from Joe.

I squeezed too hard, flattening the ball of soft cream and had to reroll. I had half a mind to confront him but knew he'd only tell me to mind my own business and stay out of what didn't concern me.

The bell over the door jingled. I jumped, dropping the cream on the floor. While Ruby and Mabel argued over who should enter first, I smiled and wiped my hands on my apron.

"Good morning, ladies." I stepped to the counter and leaned on my elbows. Experience told me it'd take them awhile to decide on their weekly two-pound box to take to their ladies auxiliary club.

The two perused the display after greeting me. "I think we should go with the maple creams. The girls really love them." Ruby folded her arms.

"We always get those." Mabel frowned. "Let's go with chocolate-covered orange peel and pineapple. Broaden our horizons."

"Why change something if there's nothing wrong with it?"

"Why don't I pack an assortment?" I asked the same question every week and waited for the usual answer.

"If we get an assortment," Ruby spoke up, "we'll get some that we won't like. No one will eat them. Waste not, want not." Mabel nodded in agreement.

"Here's a great idea. Why don't the two of you pick the assortment?" I waited for the next line.

Same thing every week. Same as clockwork, but I believed I loved the game as much as they did.

"Summer, you know we can't agree if we pick an assortment." Mabel plunked her oversize purse on the counter. "You have way too many choices."

The bell announced another customer, and I left the two friends-slash-archenemies to hash it out. Their argument ended when they turned with me, and we watched Mason White step into the store.

His normally immaculate hair stuck out in messy spikes. Wrinkles and grease marked his linen trousers.

Alarmed, I moved from behind the counter. "Are you all right?"

He shook his head and sagged against the café table in front of the window. "Minor accident." He waved a hand in my direction. "I'll be fine in a moment. A drink of water would be nice."

Ruby shoved through the waist-high saloon doors that separated the work area from the front of the store. "I'll get it. Summer, you see to the boy."

I helped Mason into a chair then peeked out the front window. "Where's your car?"

"The highway." He leaned his head onto folded arms.

"Um." I chewed my lower lip. "Why'd you come all the way into town instead of waiting for emergency vehicles?" I peered closer at him. "Did you hit your head?" I held up two fingers. "How many fingers am I holding up?"

Mason slapped my hand away. "Fine. I lied. I wasn't in an accident. Not exactly."

"Then why do you look like that?" Ruby plopped a plastic cup of water in front of him, sloshing some onto the table.

"I'm a wreck since Renee's murder. I haven't eaten. I haven't slept. Bill Olson wants to kill me. Then that old woman dying." He ran his hands through his hair. "Someone set my toolshed on fire. The whole town thinks I'm a murderer."

"Not the whole town." Mabel sat in the chair across from him. "If they did, they'd probably tar and feather you."

Mason paled beneath his salon tan.

Mabel guffawed. "I'm just joshing you. We don't do that anymore. You still haven't told us why you came here."

He looked to me for help. "I don't want to talk to you two. Not with y'all working for the paper."

Mabel's eyes gleamed as she leaned forward. "This is off the record, sonny."

"Sure it is." I took Mason by the arm and helped him to his feet. "Go on home, Mason. I'll stop by your place when I leave here." No way was I going to let Ruby and Mabel know that Mason had "hired" me to help find Renee's murderer.

Then the whole town would know.

He whispered in my ear as I pushed him out the door. "I've found out something."

My heart leaped. The day wouldn't pass fast enough.

***

"Okay, Mason. Tell." I sat across the kitchen table from him, nursing a tall glass of diet cola. At least the man had the presence of mind to clean himself up. He again looked like the Mason I knew. "What did you find out?"

He gave me a crooked smile. "Someone bashed me in the head this morning as I walked to my car. Left me lying in the dirt. They would've most likely finished me off if the garbage truck hadn't come by."

"Did you see who did it?"

"No. Got me from behind. I went in to see you as soon as I came to my senses."

"No offense, Mason, but it doesn't help me much." I ran a finger down the condensation of my glass, leaving swirling

patterns. "You said you found something out."

"Have you done any better?"

I jerked my head up at his sharp tone. Joe's voice in my head about jeopardizing the investigation made me choose my words carefully. "I'm getting there." I leaned forward.

"But there was a note left on Edna's body that leads me to believe that the males paired with the murdered females are now in jeopardy. That would be you, Hubert, and Lewis Anderson."

He folded his hands behind his head and stared past my left shoulder so intensely that I couldn't help but glance in

that direction. Nothing. Mason licked his lips. "Guess I'd best take a vacation then."

"You can't leave during a murder investigation, Mason." Joe would kill me.

"I'm not staying here to join the ranks of victims." He surged to his feet. "I've got a place in the mountains." He grabbed a pen from the counter and scribbled an address on a napkin. "If your cousin needs to reach me, I'll be here. I don't need to ask you not to give the address to anyone else, do I?"

"I'm not stupid."

"No, Summer, you aren't." He cupped my cheek, giving me a tender look. "If you weren't so wrapped up in Ethan, you and I could've had something. You're a looker. Inside and out. Wish I had what you have. That strength." He dropped a kiss on my forehead and bolted from the room.

I prayed I hadn't just let a killer dash from the room. I wished I'd had time to tell him my strength came from God. Somehow, despite his bravado, often cloying attempts at charm, and obvious lies about how much he cared for Renee, I still believed Mason innocent.

Please, God, don't let Joe throw me in jail for letting the man go.

A clock in another room chimed six o'clock, and I rose. An engine roared to life from the front of the house, and I looked out the window to the sight of Mason racing down the highway in his red Porsche. I sighed and grabbed my purse.

Back home, Aunt Eunice had left a note on the kitchen table informing me that she and Uncle Roy had gone to the movies and not to wait up for them. I smiled. They'd be home at least an hour before I went to bed. They hadn't gone to a late show in at least ten years.

After playing a quick game of hide-and-seek with Truly, I grabbed a bag of chips, poured myself another diet cola, then dumped my notes from the tote bag onto the table. Over the crunching of the chips, I tried wrapping my mind around my lack of clues.

Truly begged at my feet, her eyes imploring me for a taste of salty potato chip. Trashcan took up what looked like permanent residence smack in the middle of my stack of papers and refused to budge at the wave of my hand. Instead, the little imp pawed back.

I twirled a pencil and resorted back to thinking. Renee. . . dead. Edna. . .same. Mason. . .on a forced vacation. Sherry. . . missing. Hubert, Lewis, and Larry. . .Something nagged at the back of my brain with those three. Then there was Bill Olson. Angry, hurt, and with a strong enough motive to commit murder. My gut told me Sherry was at the center of it all, but where was the woman?

I leaned back in the chair, balancing on the back legs. If I only had the skills of Nancy Drew, Miss Marple, Sherlock Holmes, even dear Dr. Watson. At this point, I'd take the wacky crime-solving talents of Scooby-Doo.

Come on, Lord. What am I missing?

The phone rang, startling me. The chair tilted. I squeaked. Trashcan leaped from the table, scattering my notes. Truly slid under the table. My arms wind-milled as I reached, without success, for the table to steady me. Over the commotion came the musical melody of the doorbell.

256

33

I grabbed the phone as I crashed to the hard wooden floor. "Hello?"

"Summer?"

"Hi, Ethan." I grunted in pain as I struggled to my feet.

"Are you all right?"

"I fell. Let me. . .catch my breath." I set the phone down and bent over against the pain in my side where I'd landed on the arm of the chair. By the time I got back to Ethan, he'd hung up. I knew him well enough to know he was on his way over. My knight in shining armor.

I shuffled, hunched over, to answer the still-ringing doorbell. I yanked it open to the sight of Bill Olson, finger poised over the button to push again.

"Please stop with the bell." I glared at him through the screen.

"You weren't answering."

"You didn't give me time." I limped onto the porch. "What can I help you with, Bill?"

"I'm looking for Mason. I think you know where he is."

I lowered myself gingerly to the porch swing. "And how would you know that?"

"I saw your car over there today. Now he's gone." Bill folded his arms and leaned against the railing. "Don't let yourself fall into the same trap as Renee."

Despite what I feared might be bruised ribs, anger rose in me, quickening my breath, and my face heated. "I'm engaged to be married, Bill."

"She was engaged, too."

"I'm not Renee."

His eyes narrowed. "All women are the same. You can't trust any of them."

"When did you get back to town?" I hugged one of the homemade pillows to my chest. Little protection if the man should decide to attack. *Ethan, where are you?*

"A few weeks ago. Why?"

"Where have you been?" He'd had plenty of time to release his frustrations in the form of murder. I clutched my pillow tighter.

"Helping my mom with repairs around the house." His eyes shone in the falling dusk. "It wasn't until a neighbor saw Renee and Mason together that I found out the truth."

He pounded the railing post. "She'd come over, play the loving fiancée, then run off to his traitorous arms."

"That's no reason to want to kill Mason."

"Who said—"

Ethan's truck roared up the driveway. He burst from the cab and dashed to the porch. "What's going on here? If you've touched her, Bill, I'll—"

Bill held up his hands. "Slow down. I haven't laid a finger on her."

You've got to love a man who comes to your rescue with such passion.

"I'm fine, Ethan. I fell out of the chair when the phone rang. When I went back to explain it to you, you'd already hung up. Bill rang the doorbell at the same time."

"Aw man." Ethan held out a hand. "I'm sorry. Summer said she was hurt, then I see you standing over her. . ."

"No problem." Bill returned the handshake. "I thought maybe she would know where Mason is. Seems the man's disappeared. Cherish what you've got here, Ethan. A faithful woman."

With those words, he marched down the steps and disappeared down the highway.

Ethan joined me on the swing and slung an arm around my shoulders. "Are you all right?"

I nodded. "Just bruised. Something about that man seems off, doesn't it?"

"A bit." He pulled me closer, and I snuggled into his warmth. "He's grieving over Renee's death and betrayal. Now, what have you been up to?"

"Trying to make leeway on this case. I'm getting close, but I'm stuck. My books on spying and crime solving haven't helped much." I sighed. "I've been somewhere and seen something that should make it all come together, but I just can't get ahold of it."

"It'll come to you." He laid a kiss on the top of my head.

"Mason kissed me today."

"He did, huh?"

"On the forehead. Right after I warned him that I thought he might be in danger." I lifted my head to peer at Ethan. "Aren't you even the least bit jealous?"

"Why should I be? I'm the one you're snuggling on the porch swing with."

I punched him in the upper arm. "You trust me that much?"

"With all my heart. Did you like the kiss?"

"It was on the forehead. Like a brother to a sister." I settled back against him, shifting to take the pressure off my sore tailbone. "But it would've been nice for you to get a little upset. He said the two of us could have something, if it weren't for you."

"Want me to go punch his lights out?" Ethan chuckled.

"No, Bill will take care of that if he finds him." I'd have to let Joe know where Mason had gone and that Bill was looking for him. I couldn't handle having a death on my conscience. And regardless of Bill's words to the contrary, I felt he could kill if pushed. If he hadn't done so already.

***

"Joe? Did I wake you?" Propped against pillows on my bed, I settled the phone between my shoulder and ear. "Or did I interrupt something?" I giggled. "Are you and April snuggling?"

"You know me better than that. What do you want?"

"Hello to you, too." I'd seen the two wrapped around each other. Joe didn't fool me for a minute.

"You're interrupting a movie."

"Sorry." This was harder than I thought. Best just to blurt it out. "I just wanted to let you know that Mason has gone away for a while."

Joe was silent for a minute then sighed. "Okay, you have my attention. How do you know this?"

"I saw him today, and he told me."

"What time today?"

"Around six o'clock."

"It's ten o'clock! You're just now letting me know?"

"I've been busy." I slid to a slouching position. "I really think he's innocent. I know where he is if you need him. Mason said he'd been attacked in his driveway this morning. I told him about my suspicions that the killer will start on men now."

"And you believed him?"

"He was very disheveled, Joe. Not like himself at all."

"Ethan needs to have his head examined, wanting to marry a woman like you."

"You don't have to get mean." I switched the phone to my other side. "I didn't *have* to call you. You wouldn't have known any different."

Joe muttered something.

"Watch your blood pressure. Look, if he does turn out to be the bad guy, I give you permission to arrest me again."

Truly jumped on the bed and laid her head in my lap. I twirled the long hair on her ears.

"I don't need your permission!"

"Instead of yelling at me, you should be focusing more effort on catching the Conscience of

Mountain Shadows. That's what I've decided to call the killer. Catchy, isn't it? I'll have to let Ruby know so she can print it in the paper. Have you noticed he's only killed those having affairs?"

"Edna Mobley wasn't having an affair."

"A *love* affair, Joe." Sometimes my cousin could be dense.

"You're having a love affair."

My face heated. "No, I'm not! Not the kind they were. I'm a virtuous woman. Just ask Bill Olson." Well, he didn't say virtuous, but faithful was almost the same thing.

"What's he got to do with it?"

"He's looking for Mason."

"Don't tell me you told him where to look?"

"Of course not. I played dumb."

"Easy for you. Not much acting involved."

"You're being mean again. I'm hanging up." I wanted to throw the phone across the room. Instead, I exercised self-control, carefully set it in its cradle, and pounded the mattress.

Joe's wisecrack remarks made me more determined to solve this case. I'd definitely make time to visit Larry Bell's farm again tomorrow. Right after another trip to the mortuary.

34

I rushed through making nut clusters, set the pans in front of the fan to cool, then grabbed my purse. "I'm going to see Lewis Anderson. Back in a few."

Aunt Eunice frowned then waved me on. "Don't be too long. We've got work to do."

"An hour—tops." I pushed through the back door. We had orders to fill, a wedding to plan, a killer to find. My to-do list never seemed to stop. Before I knew it, I'd pulled up to the last item on my list.

Two cars sat in the parking lot of Mountain Shadows' Funeral Home. I guessed Lewis's and his receptionist's. Wonderful. No witnesses to listen to my questioning or make smart-aleck remarks about my snooping.

The slam of my car door echoed over the quiet, sweeping lawn and adjoining cemetery. Eerie, in spite of the bright September sunlight. Even more somber when I stepped inside the building.

Plush carpet muted my footsteps, and soft music played from hidden speakers. Ambience meant to soothe, yet left me feeling very alone. I shuddered. Did anyone ever really appreciate the surroundings meant to put grieving family members at ease? I didn't think so.

I glanced around the reception area. No heavily made-up woman sat behind the desk this time.

"Hello?" I peered over the desk for a bell to push. Nothing.

Guess it would detract from the peaceful atmosphere. "Anyone here?"

"May I help you?"

I stifled a cry and whirled. The woman who'd been the receptionist for Mae Belle's funeral stared impassively at me, one perfectly tweezed eyebrow raised. Was that flawless, plastic look the result of Botox or a life of no emotion? I shook my head to redirect my thoughts.

"I'm wondering whether it would be possible to speak with Mr. Anderson?"

She gave a tiny nod. "He has no other appointments. You may go on back. He's around here somewhere." The woman turned and disappeared through a door, her back as straight as an iron rod. I self-consciously adjusted my own posture.

I decided to try his office first. The door swung open at my touch. No Lewis Anderson sat behind the immaculate desk. I couldn't resist marching over to glance at his desk planner. Two funerals. Business must be slow.

I tried the drawers. Locked. Someday, I'd have to learn to pick locks. The skill would come in handy at a time like this.

A door to my right led to an empty restroom. I turned to the office window, which looked over the grounds. No sight of Mr. Anderson. Not weeping on a bench in the garden nor striding among the tombstones. Where could the grief stricken adulterer be?

Hitching my purse more securely on my shoulder, I headed to the viewing rooms. No sign of anyone—living or dead. Just rows and rows of chairs facing an empty pedestals.

If I hadn't seen the woman-with-no-expression-lines on her face, I'd have thought I was the only person in the world. Living an episode out of a *Twilight Zone* episode. I shivered and backed away to turn toward the casket showcase room.

My ears rang from the silence. I wanted to shout, dance, sing, cry, something to prove I wasn't a wraith floating from quiet place to quiet place. Casket lids lay open to reveal the plush insides.

I squinted and shuffled toward the farthest one, glanced inside, jumped back, and screamed. Lewis Anderson's eyes popped open, and he gave a shriek of his own.

"What are you doing? I thought you were dead." I clapped a hand over my mouth and staggered back.

"Taking a nap." He sat up. "These caskets are comfortable, and nobody bothers me. Usually."

"I wouldn't imagine so." I waited while he unfolded his lanky body and climbed out. If I wasn't convinced of his oddity before, I was now.

Lewis straightened his ink-colored suit jacket, slipped his feet into nearby shoes, then towered over me. "Did you need me for something? Lose another family member?"

"No, I'd like to ask you a couple of questions." I folded my arms. "Where were you yesterday morning?"

"What time?"

I cringed as I realized I hadn't asked what time someone had bashed Mason in the head. "Uh, before ten."

Lewis raised his eyebrows. "Sleeping, then I had breakfast, then I came to work. There's quite a time frame there, Miss Meadows."

"Have you seen Sherry Grover since the tornado?"

"Who? Oh, you mean the lady who worked for my Mae Belle. No, I haven't. Is she missing?" He glanced toward the door. "Would you like to stroll around the garden as we talk?"

I glanced at the empty caskets, envisioned myself inside one, and nodded. A shiver ran down my spine as we stepped into the sunshine, and I gulped a breath of the fresh air. A car sped down the nearby highway, reaffirming the fact that I wasn't alone in the world with creepy mortician Lewis Anderson.

He lowered himself to a concrete bench and patted the empty space beside him. "From your questions, I gather you're no closer to finding Mae Belle's killer."

"How well did you know Edna Mobley?" No way was I going to let one of my prime suspects know how much information I did, or didn't, possess.

"The dead lady from your aunt and uncle's party? Not well, I'm afraid. I haven't heard whether Hubert plans on using my services or not. It's been two days. He needs to make plans. Edna had no family. Poor man. Seems we've both lost someone we love."

"Don't forget Renee. Two men professed to love her."

Lewis shrugged. "Not the same, I'm afraid. My Mae Belle was a lady of the highest caliber. Not in the same league as Renee at all."

"Mae Belle was dating a married man, Mr. Anderson. You. I don't think that qualifies her as virtuous woman of the year."

His gaze hardened and focused on me with an icy glare that belied the thin-lipped smile he gave me. "Yes, we had our obstacles to overcome." He stood. "I'm afraid I have work to do, Miss Meadows. Have a nice day." Lewis spun and stalked away.

Seemed I'd touched a nerve, and Lewis Anderson moved up a notch on my suspect list. Beneath his calm demeanor lurked a crazy person. No sane man would take naps in a coffin.

I rose and headed to the parking lot. My heart skipped a beat to see Hubert, head down, making his way to the front door of the building. "Mr. Smith!"

The man actually grimaced when he spotted me then stopped and forced a smile to his face. "Do you need a follow-up
appointment?"

"No, thank you. My teeth are fine. How are *you* doing?" People didn't make dental appointments at funeral homes, did they?

He took a deep breath. "I'm okay. Running errands and. . .making arrangements."

"Is there anything I can do?"

Hubert sniffed. "The night Edna died, we'd had a fight. I'd dragged her into the woods for a little, um, well, you get the idea. She said it'd be too embarrassing. Too many people around. Someone could catch us. I said the thrill would keep us young. She stormed off in a huff."

I gnawed the inside of my cheek before answering. "I thought the two of you were playing a game. Hide-and-seek."

"She hid. I searched. Really Miss Meadows, I've business to attend to. And not pleasant business at that."

"I just spoke with Mr. Anderson, and he said he had no appointments today. He also seemed surprised that you haven't approached him sooner about making arrangements. Are the two of you friends?"

"Good day, Miss Meadows. I'm here to plan a funeral. Nothing more." Hubert pushed through the swinging doors and left me standing like a wayward child outside.

Another wasted day of questioning. I glanced at my watch. Aunt Eunice would be furious. I'd been gone longer than planned.

***

"I'm sorry," I said rushing into the store. "I'll stay late tonight and catch up."

Aunt Eunice inclined her head toward the counter. "Mail came."

I paused. My heart pounded harder than a rock-and-roll drummer. I proceeded with leaden steps to the basket where we stashed our incoming mail. Aunt Eunice's tone told me I wouldn't like what I'd find.

Sticking higher than the other envelopes rose a navy blue one with my name and address in letters cut from a magazine. Again, I remembered where I'd seen enough magazines for someone to have a seemingly unending supply.

"Call Joe. Ask him to come over at once. Tell him I think I know who the killer is."

35

"Not a wise idea." A synthesized sound came from the direction of the door. Aunt Eunice gasped and wrapped her fingers around a wooden spoon. To use as a weapon? I glanced around for something of my own.

The wraith from Saturday night floated into the candy store and turned the dead bolt on the door. He seemed to glide. His feet were hidden beneath drapes of fabric. A black-gloved hand pointed a gun in our direction.

"Touch the phone, utter another word, even look at each other, and I'll use this. I prefer a weapon less noisy, but a gun works in a pinch. Miss Meadows, come with me, if you please."

Thankfully, I stood partially hidden behind a waist-high wall where I could scribble my suspect's name on a slip of paper before stepping out. I opened my mouth to say something but clamped it shut at another wave from the gun. This time

in Aunt Eunice's direction.

"Leave my aunt here. She isn't involved in this." *Please, God, don't let him shoot her.*

"If you don't tell her your suspicions, she'll stay uninvolved. I have no desire to harm such a virtuous woman as your aunt."

My gaze fell on a pan of melted chocolate. Quick as I could, I grabbed the pan and flung the contents where the wraith's face should've been.

He actually had the gall to laugh at me. "I'm wearing a mask, super sleuth. Anything else you want to throw?" He shook his head, sending drops of melted goodness to the floor. "Let's go."

With another wave of his weapon, he ushered me out the back door and into the trunk of a dark-colored sedan.

"Wait." I held up my hand. Maybe if I stalled him long enough, someone would see us. It isn't every day someone draped in black walks down the street. "How'd you get into the store without being seen?"

"Elementary, my dear Watson. We'll talk later." He slammed the trunk closed.

Idiot. He didn't even tie my hands or gag me. I kicked against the metal above me and screamed as loud as I could.

Wait. Did his trunk have an inside release? I felt the area around me.

Sunlight blinded me when he opened the trunk. "Almost forgot. Thank you for reminding me." He clunked me in the head with the butt of his pistol. My last thought before the lights went out was that I'd correctly identified Mae Belle's murderer.

***

I woke in a dark place that smelled of wet earth. My head ached, my stomach roiled, I was cold, and

I needed to use the restroom. "Great. Wonderful. Once again, I'm thrust down a hole."

"Who's there? Is that Summer Meadows?"

"Sherry?" I crawled toward the voice. "Where are we?"

"I think it's a root cellar. Wherever we are, the place has dirt walls."

Without being invited, I sat close enough to her for our shoulders to touch. She might not be one of my closest friends, but she *was* company in a very dark, scary place. And I had no qualms about sharing her body warmth.

Even if it became apparent she really did hunt bats. I still wanted to know what kind of tools she kept in her bag. "But *where* are we?"

"Somewhere on Larry's farm, I think. I'm not sure. He bonked me in the head, and I woke up here."

"Sounds familiar. You're Lola, aren't you?"

I felt her turn toward me. "Yes."

"I figured that out and that Larry is the one murdering people, but what I can't get is why." I scoffed. "Actually, there's a lot of why. Why the computer scam? Why is Larry killing people? I call him the Conscience of Mountain Shadows. Why is he picking on me?"

"I can answer some of your questions. The others you'll have to ask him when he comes for his visit. The man's completely nuts." She shifted. "The scam is exactly that. A way to get money. Mae Belle didn't pay enough to get me out of my Internet gambling debts, so I sold love over the Internet."

I remembered the letters I'd found in her apartment. "Which is really gross, by the way."

She laughed. "But it pays well. Mae Belle found out, went to warn Larry, and he got mad. Snapped, from the looks of it. Said she ruined his life and should have left well enough alone. That it wasn't a scam, but true love. Then he went on to say he was going to cleanse Mountain Shadows of immoral people, starting with the women.

"At least that's what he told me. I tried to run away by using the twister as cover but wrecked instead. Sorry about your car. Larry grabbed me, and here I am. I think my arm's broken from when I ran the car into the building, but he won't call a doctor, the big jerk."

"Are you talking about me, my love?" A flashlight clicked on and shone from above us. Larry moved the beam from Sherry's face to mine. "Ah, you're awake." He lit an oil lamp, lowered a ladder, and joined us to place the light at his feet.

"Always." Sherry's voice softened, taking on a husky tone. If I hadn't seen her in person, I'd never have known it was her. "Did you bring dinner?"

"Fried chicken, mashed potatoes, and biscuits." Larry smoothed an old quilt on the dirt-packed floor. "Join me, sweetheart."

I made a move forward. Larry whipped a pistol from the pocket of his sweats fast enough to put Marshal Dillon to shame and pointed it in my direction. "I don't even want to know you're here."

"I need to use the restroom."

"There's a bucket in the corner."

"You have got to be kidding!" *Gross.*

His glare silenced me. He turned back to Sherry. "I'm sorry to keep you down here, Lola, but until you see the error of your ways, I must."

"I have, Larry. I promise. I'm a new woman. If you let me out, I can prove it to you."

He shook his head and took a bite out of a chicken leg. My stomach growled. The icy look from Larry made me press against the wall and hug my knees. If I could get Sherry to join with me, the two of us could take him, even with her injured arm. I'd taken at least five self-defense classes. I'd read books.

"What are you going to do with me?" I asked.

Larry sighed and laid the chicken bone on a napkin. "I can see that you won't allow me to eat my dinner in peace. I haven't decided what to do with you, actually. You weren't on my list of immoral people. I tried to warn you away from snooping, but you obviously can't take a hint. Now I find myself in quite a predicament. If I kill you, how will I ever look Ethan in the face?"

He shook his head. "How did you find out it was me?"

"That labyrinth made from stacks of magazines in your house."

He made a sound deep in his throat. "You shouldn't have been in my house."

"I have to admit, you're good. It took me awhile." At least I'd figured it out before he put the gun to my head. Usually, that's when everything became clear. "I'd like to know why, though. As long as I'm here."

He sighed again. "I'm a broken man. My heart is shattered, and I'm struggling to repair it. Lola is going to help. She's made me many wonderful promises. I'm confident I can turn her from the error of her ways. The others were better disposed of. Rubbish. All of them."

Guess the man hadn't learned the truth about everyone made in God's image. Worthy of life and love, no matter their mistakes. And I thought *I* could be judgmental.

"How did you know I'd find out it was you?" I crossed my legs.

"Mae Belle started acting suspicious. I thought she might leave clues with someone close to her. I tried to get rid of her before she had time, but then you hired her to plan your wedding. After your solving those other cases, I knew it was a matter of time. Unless I could turn you away. You don't scare very easy. An admirable trait."

He took another bite of chicken. "You do realize the woman wasn't very good at parties, don't you? You would've wasted your money."

The casualness of the conversation made my blood run cold. My bladder ached. I squeezed my legs together. "Why didn't you kill me along with the rest? And why the women? Were you going to start on the men?"

"You ask too many questions." He rose. "I've lost my appetite. The two of you can finish the chicken." Keeping his gun trained on us, Larry climbed the ladder and pulled it up after himself.

"You must have a death wish," Sherry said as I returned from using the bucket. She dug into the potatoes with a plastic fork. "Larry doesn't like questions, and you have a lot of them."

I joined her on the quilt. "If I'm going to be stuck in this dirt hole, I'd like some answers." I plucked a chicken breast from the basket. "Besides, he wants to do away with immorality, but he's content to keep 'Lola' locked in a root cellar? I'm not buying it."

"He loves me. What can I say?" Sherry shrugged then winced. Most likely from the pain in her arm. "Larry admires Ethan. His faith, his work ethic. Since you're engaged to marry Ethan, Larry obviously wanted to avoid killing you. I told you the guy's nuts.

"He's been scorned too many times and *really* dislikes women. He told me once during our e-mail chats that the world was full of loose women leading foolish men astray. Except me. For some reason he thinks I'm worth saving. The crazy man actually believes all the lies I've told him."

"You don't think so?"

"Think what?"

"That you're worth saving?"

She shrugged and lifted a chicken leg from the basket. "I've not been the best of people, Summer. If I see an opportunity, I take it. Regardless of who may get hurt in the process."

"Like taking my car."

"Exactly. But the wreck wasn't my fault." She waved the chicken bone in my direction. "Remember that. Mother Nature had a hand in it."

"There's a way for you to be made new."

This was the best chicken I'd ever tasted. Maybe because I was starving, but I dug into the food like it was my last meal. Which possibly, it could be.

"If you're talking about God, forget it. I've heard the stories. Besides, what would a squeaky-clean girl like you know about anything?"

Sherry tossed the bone into the corner of the cellar. "If you do get out of here, you'd better grab ahold of that man of yours and never let go. It's his reputation that's kept Larry from killing you."

"I'm not squeaky clean. I've got issues."

Sherry laughed. "Like what? How you're going to get chocolate out of your designer pants? Or what shade of lipstick to wear?"

Did people really think I was that shallow? That self-absorbed? I'd tried hard over the last few months to dispel the thoughts that I was an empty-headed, spoiled little girl.

I sighed and dropped my half-eaten chicken back into the empty basket. "I've spent my life judging people by their outside, instead of their heart. If I didn't get my way, I'd stomp my feet and pout. I blamed myself for my parents' death." I lifted my chin and peered at Sherry's face. "Despite my faith in God's ability to handle any situation I found myself in, I've wanted to retain control. Except lately. I've been doing better."

"Well, your problems still don't add up to the things I've done. And now, it's all about to come to an end. If Larry doesn't kill me, I'll be going to jail. But it's been one wild, fun ride."

Sherry leaned forward and lowered the wick on the lamp. "We've got to save the oil. Larry won't be back until breakfast, and he only fills the lamp for about an hour of light."

"We'll be stuck in the dark?" I jumped to my feet.

"For hours."

My heart leaped into my throat, beating a primitive rhythm of fear. "Are there rats in here? Bugs?"

"Scared? Afraid your God won't save you?" Sherry whipped the blanket from beneath me, scattering the remains of our dinner, and knocking me flat on my tush.

"Larry didn't leave the blanket last night. I almost froze to death. He must have forgotten to take it in the middle of all your questions."

The way she yanked that blanket, I doubted her arm was broken. Maybe bruised, or a ploy to gain sympathy. Something I had in short supply. I rubbed my aching tailbone. "Yes, I'm scared, but God promises to watch over those who love Him."

Sherry wrapped the quilt around her shoulders and scooted to place her back against the wall. "Sure He does. That's why you're locked down here. Or are you going to feed me that hogwash about how God didn't put you down here?"

"He didn't. Larry did, and I ain't dead yet, as the saying goes. I'm sorry your heart is hardened against God, but I still believe He'll get us out of here."

I stood and stared at the trapdoor over our heads. A thin beam of light outlined the edges of the weathered wood. Was it indoor light or moonbeams? "If you let me stand on your shoulders, I might be able to push that open."

Sherry stared for a moment at the trapdoor. "I guess it's worth a try." With a groan, she pushed to her feet, letting the quilt fall into a pile on the ground. "Let's do this while the light lasts. And make it quick. Even as little as you are, this isn't going to feel good on my arm."

Sherry stood about a head taller than me and squatted to enable me to climb onto her shoulders. Having been imprisoned down here for a couple of days, she smelled rank.

"What are you, twelve feet tall?"

She laughed. "Not that tall, but I am full-figured. Plenty of handholds for you."

I held my breath and thanked the Lord no one could see my ungainly ascent as I attempted to climb without her greasy hair brushing against me. With my short legs finally wrapped around her neck, Sherry attempted to guide me to stand on her shoulders.

"Take my hand. Use me as balance."

I swayed and flailed my arms. "Give me your other hand, too. I'm going to fall!"

"No, you aren't. Be still. Besides, I told you I was injured. Weren't you a cheerleader? I seem to remember you getting tossed in the air by a couple of Barbie dolls."

"That was a long time ago, and you weren't on the squad. You have no idea how to be a stable base for me."

"How hard can it be? I'm twice your size. Just hang on."

"Stop." I reached for the wall. "Let me use the wall as leverage."

We teetered and swayed our way over until I leaned against the damp dirt enclosure. "Okay, I'm ready to stand. On the count of three. Okay? One. Two—"

With her good hand pressed against the heels of my feet, Sherry heaved. I tottered forward then backward and grasped for the wall. My fingernails raked as I fell, leaving them filled with dirt. I hit the ground hard enough to knock the breath out of me.

On my descent, I managed to hit the lamp, shattering the glass and spilling the oil. The quilt went up in flames, highlighting a leaping Sherry as she demonstrated a shadowy dance in order to avoid the hungry fire.

"You didn't—wait until—I said—three."

"Just great, Summer!" Sherry grabbed a corner of fabric that wasn't burning and whacked the blanket against the ground. "Now we'll have no light, and the fire will burn up all our oxygen. We're going to suffocate."

With tears of pain in my eyes, I clutched my stomach and fought to catch my breath. This latest escapade of mine was too physical for my taste. Falling over in chairs, getting dragged from cars, now this. I seriously contemplated giving up the crime-solving business.

Only after the last of the fire flickered out, leaving us in darkness, could I smile. God always provided a way.

My absentmindedness might have finally amounted to something.

My cell phone, with its new GPS tracker, was in my purse. In the trunk of Larry's car. The car that brought me here.

36

"This is what hell will be like." I wasn't aware I'd spoken out loud until Sherry cursed.

"Would you lay off the religious garbage? We're in dire straits here."

"All the more reason to call on God."

I pushed to a sitting position then crawled until I found Sherry. Again, I sat as close to her as humanly possible without sitting on her. Our dirt prison grew as cool as a refrigerator.

"Hell will be dark and absent of life. All we're lacking is the gnashing of teeth."

"Summer, I'm warning you."

"How long have I been down here?"

"Most of a day. You were unconscious for a while when Larry dropped you in."

"What's taking them so long?" A whole day! Surely, Aunt Eunice called Joe and Ethan the moment Larry ushered me out of Summer Confections. How long did it take to trace someone? Did Larry leave us and drive somewhere else?

I battled the despair threatening to suffocate me. Never having been a fan of the dark, and now locked into a place that smelled of dirt, burnt quilting, and the contents of our toilet bucket, I struggled to control my breathing. *Okay, God, I'm handing my fear over to You. On the count of three. One, two, three—*

"Did you hear that?"

I leaned forward, straining. There. A whine and scratching at the door above us. Dirt rained on my head. "It's Truly. I'm here! Ethan!" *Thank You, Lord, that my silly puppy likes to play hide-and-seek.*

A gun boomed over us, and I gasped. Running to stand beneath the faint glow from the door, I jumped, trying to stretch my five-foot-two-inch frame. Another gunshot. *God, help them! Please don't let Ethan be hurt.*

I whirled toward Sherry. "I'll hurt your lover boy if something happens to Ethan!"

She came to stand beside me. "Way to rely on your God. Got a lot of faith showing right now."

I bit back another retort. She was right. Ethan was in God's hands. Hands stronger than any bullet that might be aimed toward him. I fell to my knees and prayed harder than I'd ever prayed before.

Despite what sounded like a gunfight in the Old West, peace descended over me, and I sat down to wait for whatever the outcome.

Sherry joined me. "I can't picture your fiancé shooting anyone. Guess the police found us."

"Yep. Joe has shot people before. Your time in here is almost over."

"I'm glad. My plan didn't work anyway. I'm just as broke as when I started, and loan sharks can't get to me in prison."

"You know, Sherry, in a roundabout way, you're responsible for several people's deaths. If you hadn't played with Larry's affections, he might not have snapped."

"You're probably right. I've thought about that the last few days. Being shut down here doesn't allow for much more than thinking. Nothing can be done about it now."

I reached over and took her hand. "I'll pray for you while you're in jail. I'll pray that you'll finally see the light."

"It can't hurt." She slipped her hand free. Someone shouted something over a bullhorn that I couldn't decipher. I prayed Joe would be able to talk Larry into the open without anyone being killed. Truly's scratching at the door had stopped, and I hoped my wiry little terrier was okay.

Time crawled before Truly again scratched at the trapdoor. The pale light of dusk washed over us when the door lifted. The ladder slid down with a thud.

"Summer!"

"Ethan!"

I bolted up, banging my shin on the wooden rung of the ladder as I shimmied up and launched myself into the best place I'd ever wanted to be. The safety of Ethan's arms. I jumped up and wrapped my arms and legs around him and washed his face with kisses.

Truly yipped and jumped around Ethan's legs. I laughed and slid down to pet her. "You are such a good girl. Yes, you are."

"Once we reached Larry's farm, Truly led us right to you. Good thing you taught her that game."

"Larry started shooting. Warnings mostly. He didn't hit anyone. I think he'd pretty much given up."

Joe marched over and pulled me into a hug. "Cuz, you've got to stop doing this. You're killing me. We can't keep saving you every few months."

"Thank you, Joe, for putting that tracker on my phone. That is how y'all found me, isn't it?" I returned Joe's hug and headed back to Ethan.

"Yep. Pretty smart, your leaving your purse in Larry's trunk." Joe grinned. "Although I think he drove around most of the county before coming home for the night. Stupid signal bounced all over the place."

My face heated. "That was an accident."

He laughed. "I never thought otherwise. And it didn't hurt that you wrote Larry's name on the counter." He turned to help Sherry out of the cellar. "Ma'am, if you'll come with me." Joe led her to a squad car

Larry peered from the window of a cruiser parked in front of his house. His head turned to follow Sherry. I was glad to see the love-struck man still lived. I'd add him to my prayer list. He'd have plenty of time to come to terms with God. Larry Bell was going to be in jail for a very long time.

"Are you all right?"

I turned to look into my beloved's face. "I've never been better."

Ethan caressed my cheek. "Do you think you can stay out of trouble long enough to plan our wedding?"

I wrapped my arms around his neck. "I think so."

***

"You look gorgeous." April straightened my veil. "Only someone with your tiny figure could wear that dress. I hope I look half as beautiful on my wedding day."

I ran a hand down the satin skirt and glanced at the bouquet of midnight blue roses in my hand. Uncle Roy had searched everywhere for a nursery with the dark purple roses in bloom. Anything for my special day, he'd said.

April Fool's Day arrived on sun rays, blue skies, and puffy clouds. Flowers bloomed around the grounds of the church as if God smiled, especially for me, on my wedding day.

"Have you seen Ethan?" I raised a trembling hand to tuck a stray curl beneath my veil.

"Afraid he'll skip out on you?"

"Never."

"Oh my goodness!" Aunt Eunice slipped through the door, her eyes brimming with tears. "You look like you've stepped from the pages of a magazine."

I turned and held out my arms. "I feel like a princess. A true princess of the King."

"How's my girl?" Uncle Roy followed Aunt Eunice. In his hand he held a thin, narrow white jewelers box. "I've brought you something." He opened the lid and lifted a delicate silver bracelet. "Entwined roses. To match your ring."

Tears sprang to my eyes, and I found myself doing the silly pageant-girl hand flutter to my eyes. "Put it on me." I held out my arm. "Can this day get any more perfect?"

Uncle Roy crooked his arm. "I know how it can. There's a very nervous young man waiting for you, dressed in a monkey suit."

I placed my arm in his. "Then let's not keep him waiting."

The organ struck up the wedding march as Joe pushed open the doors. The sun shone through the stained glass windows lighting my way with rays of color. Ethan smiled at me from the other end of the white carpet runner. I glanced toward heaven and blew God a kiss, before taking the first step toward my soon-to-be husband.

Enjoy the first chapter of book four, Maui Macadamia Madness.

The plane dropped fifty feet. A woman screamed.

I closed my eyes and gripped Ethan's arm like a pit bull to a steak. I—Summer Meadows, uh, Banning, having been married less than twelve hours, I tended to forget my new last name—did not like to fly. Not one iota. "Whose idea was it to fly to Maui?"

Ethan laughed and pulled me as close as the armrest between us would allow. "Yours. I wanted to cruise, but you said you didn't want to leave Aunt Eunice with the store for too long."

"You should have stopped me. I was delusional." I buried my face in his shirt front. "Out of my mind with marital bliss." My stomach leaped as the plane jumped again. Please, don't let me lose my dinner. Why couldn't the airline have a direct flight to Maui instead of their having to fly a prop plane from the main island to their destination?

Ethan rubbed my head. "Did you manage to sleep? I'd hate for you to arrive in Maui with gritty eyes."

"A little. You?" I peeked up at him, wanting to run my fingers through his mussed hair. One night as his wife, and I loved him even more than before.

"Like a baby."

I'd hardly slept a wink. Something about there being nothing but air between me and the ocean kept me awake and white knuckled. Not to mention the man behind us who snored like a bulldog with sinus problems. "I'll sleep once we reach the Bed and Breakfast in Kihei." I grinned. "But hopefully not too much."

Ethan bent and gave me one of his heart-stopping, lip-searing kisses. Normally, people might think getting married on April Fool's Day a bad omen, but not me. I thought it funny and unique. Just like me and my new husband. Doing things out of the ordinary kept life interesting.

I loosened my grip on his arm and grabbed the arm rests as the plane began its descent. Fun with the most handsome man on God's green earth, no dead bodies or internet scams, no one shooting at me, all pointed to the most perfect ten days a woman could hope to have.

The plane landed smoothly. Passengers stood and reached for their carry-on bags before the fasten seatbelt light blinked off. I stepped aside and let Ethan handle ours while I tried to peer around people and out the windows. From what I could see, the airport looked like any other one I had been in. A squat white building on a tarmac. I sighed and took my makeup bag. Ethan placed his free hand on the curve of my lower back, sending delicious tremors up my spine, and steered me off the plane.

We made our way to baggage claim, waited until our suitcases arrived, then headed outside to the van that would take us to Wahine's Bed and Breakfast. Lovely young women, arms loaded with leis, welcomed us with "Aloha." The fragrant scent of flowers and ocean filled the air. I breathed deep, certain I was as close to heaven as a woman could get and still be on earth.

Excitement rose like champagne bubbles and colored the day rosy. I fairly skipped to the transport van and showed the driver our registration papers while Ethan lugged the bags. Strong as he was, he groaned under the weight. I tended to over pack, as evidenced by the extra fees for the luggage weight and extra bags. But, a girl had to be prepared for anything.

Three other couples joined us on the van ride, two obviously married, and one that ignored each other. Either they were a couple angry with each other or strangers. Maybe the beauty and romance of Maui would soothe whatever ailed them.

As the driver moved to close the door, another man ran up, shouting for us to wait. The driver scowled and motioned for the man to sit in the front passenger seat. Once everyone and their bags were secure, he slid behind the wheel.

"This is it." I glanced at Ethan. "We're really here. On our honeymoon. On Maui."

He grinned back and squeezed my hand.

"Yes, we are."

"Oooh, honeymooners." A plump woman sitting in front of us beamed over the back of the seat. Her greying brown hair was clipped back in flower barrettes and the colors on her tent-of-a-housedress would blind a man with no eyes. "I'm Sharon Aldrich, this is my husband, Ron. We're celebrating our twenty-fifth wedding anniversary. We spent our honeymoon here, too."

Her husband, a round, balding man, nodded and unfolded a newspaper. Sharon tapped the other couple. "Since we're all going to be spending the next few days together, we should get acquainted."

The other couple looked to be in their mid-twenties. "We're Bruce and Maryann Franklin," the young man said. "On our honeymoon." He landed a loud smack on his wife's lips. She reddened and cupped his face. They rubbed noses like a couple of Eskimos.

Sharon turned to the last two. "And you two are?"

"Not married and strangers." The woman pulled a lipstick and compact from her purse. She reminded me of Ethan's ex-girlfriend, Terry Lee. Dark hair, shapely figure, legs that went on forever. I disliked her on the spot. "I'm Susan Wood, here on vacation."

"I'm David Hatcher. Business." He was good looking in a California surfer kind-of-way with longish sun-bleached brown hair and brown eyes. His gaze flicked over Susan's shoulder and landed, for a moment, on the back of the front passenger's head.

"And you, sir?" Sharon leaned forward, trying to gain the attention of the man in front.

"Here on business." He continued to stare out the window. A gold Rolex watch winked from his left wrist.

"Do you know each other?" Sharon motioned between the man and David. When David shook his head and the other man didn't reply, she shrugged and turned back to Ethan and me. "The other honeymooners?"

"Summer and Ethan Banning." I reached out my hand to shake hers. "From Arkansas."

"Well, well," Susan simpered. "So am I. I thought you looked familiar. You're the wannabe sleuth from Mountain Springs. I read about you in the Arkansas River News."

"Nothing wannabe about it." I lifted my chin. "I solved three crimes." And almost died solving each one of them.

Ethan placed a restraining hand on my leg and leaned close. "We're on our honeymoon, Tinkerbell. No crime talk."

I got the warm fuzzies at the nickname he used to tease me with because of my petite size. What a turnaround from when I used to take offense. I felt the love in his words. I patted his leg. "I know." I transferred my attention to the lush greenery passing outside the window.

Wahine's Bed and Breakfast sat on a private beach, its pristine white siding a brilliant contrast to the azure sky. Off to the sides sat quaint huts with thatched roofs and cascading blossoms dripping from the eaves. Opposite the hotel, the beach sparkled like diamonds, inviting a person to indulge in an oceanic dip. I couldn't wait to sink my toes into the wet sand at the water's edge.

"Aloha!" A brown-skinned couple, him in a tropical shirt and her in a purple muumuu, held their arms wide in welcome. "Your home awaits you," the man said. "I am Larry Wahine, and this is my princess-of-a-bride, Anna."

How sweet of him to call his wife his princess. I glanced up at Ethan, who grinned and planted a kiss on my nose.

"You've been my princess from the moment I first laid eyes on you when you were a skinny, freckle-faced, twelve-year-old."

He always knew exactly what to say to heat up the water.

"We have lots of fun planned," Mr. Wahine explained. "From snorkeling to luaus, parasailing to whale watching. We hope that all of you will join in the group activities, but if not," his smile never faded. "We will guide you where you want to go. Now, to show you to your rooms. Come, follow me."

"I hope you paid attention to my reservation requests," Mr. Businessman said. "I requested a cottage set apart from the others."

"Yes, Mr. Jamison, we've set you aside as far as possible." I wasn't sure, but I would have sworn Mr. Wahine actually rolled his eyes.

"This way, Mr. and Mrs. Banning." Mrs. Wahine headed left, motioning for the other honeymooners to follow us. "Our honeymoon cottages are this way. It allows for a little more privacy." She winked and opened the door to our suite. "We do rent a few rooms in the main house, but folks tend to enjoy it out here more."

Wicker furniture and tropical fabrics welcomed us. A large basket of fruit with a platter of cheese and bread beside it sat on a coffee table. Although this was our second night as husband and wife, my face burned at sight of the king-sized bed draped with mosquito netting.

Ethan sat our bags beside the bed then moved to open the French doors. "Look at this view, Summer."

I slipped under his arm and took in the scene in front of me. Waves caressed the beach, palm trees swayed, and the last of the day's wind surfers filled the ocean with bright colors. "Paradise."

He squeezed me. "Do you want to eat in tonight, or join the others?"

"I'd like to eat right there from the fruit basket." I motioned at the small bistro table on our deck. "Do you think the Wahine's will mind?"

"I'm sure they expect it from newlyweds."

"Most likely."

"Sit while I get the basket." He moved inside. "There's a bottle of sparkling cider and one of grape juice. Which do you want?"

"The cider, please." I sat in a wicker chair and the fuschia cushions let out a *whoosh*. I set my feet on the small footstool in front of me. I could sit there every night and watch the sun go down past the water.

Especially if Ethan sat beside me. He placed the basket and tray on a wrought iron patio table, then went back inside for our drinks, leaving me to cut the bread with the knife provided.

"Look, Ethan, a box of chocolate-covered macadamia's." I lifted a white box wrapped with a sunshine yellow ribbon from the basket. I had started serving them in my store, but the nuts had a tendency to spoil so quickly, I didn't stock them as often as I would like. This was a rare treat. I opened the box, picked out a couple of pieces, and settled back to enjoy the view.

Did the natives of Hawaii ever get used to the sight of a crimson sun lowering over water painted with magenta and pumpkin, or did they take the sight for granted? I sighed and watched as the last wind surfer strolled across the beach and past the hotel.

"To us." Ethan handed me a wine glass and bent to kiss me.

"To us." I raised my glass in toast,

returned his kiss, and then transferred my attention back to the beach.

Someone ran through the deepening shadows.

"Looks like one of the guests is enjoying an early evening jog." I took a sip of my drink as he or she ran past our balcony, a dark-colored hoodie pulled over their head. I shrugged. To each their own, my Aunt Eunice always said.

With the sun setting, the weather cooled off, but not enough to warrant even a light weight jacket, at least in my opinion. The person glanced toward us. Their steps faltered as I raised my glass, then the person sprinted off.

A scream shattered the peace of the night.

298

Be sure to check out the rest of the Summer Meadows Mystery Series:

Fudge-Laced Felonies Book 1
Chocolate-Covered Crime Book 3
Maui Macadamia Madness Book 4

And her new series:
Deadly Neighbors
Advance Notice

Visit her website at www.cynthiahickey.com

ABOUT THE AUTHOR

Multi-published author Cynthia Hickey had three cozy mysteries published through Barbour Publishing, with a novella releasing in March 2013. Her first mystery, Fudge-Laced Felonies, won first place in the inspirational category of the Great Expectations contest in 2007. Her third cozy, Chocolate-Covered Crime, received a four-star review from Romantic Times. All three cozies have been re-released as ebooks through the MacGregor Literary Agency, along with a new cozy series. She has several historical romances releasing in 2013 and 2014 through Harlequin's Heartsong Presents. She lives in Arizona with her husband, one of their seven children, two dogs and two cats. She has five grandchildren who keep her busy and tell everyone they know that "Nana is a writer". Visit her website at www.cynthiahickey.com

www.ingramcontent.com/pod-product-compliance
Lightning Source LLC
Chambersburg PA
CBHW061015120726
47910CB00006B/1943